DAVID FRANKEL w
the westerly fringes
have been shortlisted
The Bristol Prize,
Tom-Gallon Trust Award, The Wiiiesuc.. ---
and the Fish Memoir Prize. His work has been
published in numerous anthologies and magazines,
and also in a chapbook by Nightjar Press. He also
writes non-fiction exploring memory and landscape.

DAVID FRANKEL

FORGETTING IS HOW WE SURVIVE

SALT
**MODERN
STORIES**

SALT

CROMER

PUBLISHED BY SALT PUBLISHING 2023

2 4 6 8 10 9 7 5 3

First published in Great Britain in 2023 by
Salt Publishing Ltd
12 Norwich Road, Cromer, Norfolk NR27 0AX United Kingdom

www.saltpublishing.com

Salt Publishing Limited Reg. No. 5293401

A CIP catalogue record for this book is available from the British Library

ISBN 978 1 78463 301 1 (Paperback edition)
ISBN 978 1 78463 302 8 (Electronic edition)

Typeset in Granjon by Salt Publishing

Printed and bound in Great Britain by Clays Ltd, St Ives plc

For Grace

Contents

Contents

Ghost Story

MORE INVESTIGATORS COME, so you tell your story again. Some believe you, others don't. Some pay, others don't. Sometimes you forget details, or the story gets muddled and you are forced to double back, retracing your steps. Sometimes you get excited as you describe what happened and, in your enthusiasm, you embellish – you are only human, after all. These variances create doubt, and you don't want to be perceived as dishonest, so you begin to consider your words more carefully. Each time you recount the facts, your delivery becomes more refined. You know, now, how to project integrity, trustworthiness, and when to pause to allow the gravity of what you are saying sink in. You understand how to present your best side to the suspicious lens of the camera.

Although you only ever wanted to tell the truth, you cannot remember what that strange mixture of feelings was like. You know only how it looked in your mind's eye the last time you recalled it. Each time you recount what happened that day, you piece it together from what you remember saying the time before, the image resolving a little more with each re-telling, its edges becoming more clearly drawn, and you are comforted by this lack of doubt. So you tell the story of what you saw again; the memory of a memory of a memory. A ghost, if you will.

Sink Rate

CAROLINE IS AWARE of the sound of a plane's engines, a distant whine on the aural horizon, growing louder, rising in pitch. Although she has come to the beach to escape the noise of the island's biggest town, the distant plane is only a minor annoyance.

As the sound grows louder, people around her begin to look for the plane in the sky. It is invisible against the glare of the sun until it appears like a sudden mirage, very close, low, moving impossibly slowly. Holiday makers on the beach pause, phones in hand, to watch the plane descend on its final, tree-skimming approach to the airport's outer marker. Three times a day, six in high season, it's a spectacle that is noted in most guidebooks.

Engine noise reflects from the water, and she feels the vibrations in her gut. It's impossible not to watch, impossible not to stand hypnotised with the other customers of the beach bar. But today the more experienced among them sense something wrong in the uneven whining of the engines, and Caroline has spent enough time in airports to know that the plane is too low. It wallows in the hot, island air as though it is treading water and then begins a ponderous bank away from the crowded beach – perhaps a rookie pilot misjudging their approach and going around for another shot.

The watchers on the beach freeze as the plane dips lower, then lower still, until its wing touches the water, gently slicing the waves. But this moment of delicacy is an illusion. The pull of that graceful curl of water is enough to pitch the plane violently. Its engines give a final scream and the fuselage quivers. It hits the sea nose-first, flipping and lurching into a cartwheel that destroys it in a vast explosion of spray and steam.

Caroline stands with the others, unable to move. It is all over in a few beats of her hammering heart, but those moments seem to have stretched out, filling her past and future. Later she will remember the sound of rain – debris and scattered spray falling back into the sea – and the beautiful rainbow that appeared briefly above the sinking sections of fuselage. She will not remember the smell of aviation fuel or the screaming of frightened children on the beach, although others will. The whole event has taken seconds. It has been captured on two-dozen cell phones. A metal tube travelling at 130 miles per hour hitting the water and breaking apart, conceding to the dreadful Newtonian certainty of action and reaction.

For everyone on board, and everyone on the beach, the path of life is altered. She is completely unharmed, but Caroline feels this change, although she is only distantly aware of it and won't be able to verbalise it until years later. 'As though,' she will tell her therapist dreamily, 'the points on a train track were switched and the train moved from one line, one set of destinations, to another.'

In the long moments following the crash, she stands, bare feet buried in the hot sand, dazzled by the sun on the bright sea. The rain of spray falls away and the silence that has closed around her fractures. She becomes aware of voices and screams. Men, locals she presumes, drag small pleasure-boats down the beach and steer them towards the sinking wreckage. Behind her, a drunken Frenchman is speaking in English, trying to sound unimpressed, 'Not the best landing I've seen.' An American nearby repeats, 'Oh my God' over and over, speaking into her mobile but giving no indication of a two-way conversation. Oh my God. Oh my God.

The heat of the sun is suddenly too much. Caroline feels sweat running down her temples and her mouth is dry. She feels the sickly sweetness of the cocktails she has been drinking rising in her throat as her entrails churn inside her. She runs, not towards the sea like the others, but to the small toilet block behind the bar where, hovering above the dirty pan and clutching her skirt around her stomach, she empties her bowels.

At the tiny, metal sink, she washes, glad of the cool water. She is trembling. Is this shock? she wonders. Nobody else from the beach is in here shaking. Disgusted at her weakness, she slaps her own face and turns to a small mirror hanging on the far wall. Her image, skin pale and glistening wet, is caught in the small, dirty oval of glass. She raises her hand to wipe it, touching the cold reflection, and it is at this moment that she recalls the woman.

As the plane began its final desperate bank and turn, she had seen a single face at a window; a woman's face, framed in the little rectangle of grey glass. In her mind, she replays the moment before the fuselage ruptured. The whole thing had been so close it was possible to see bags being flung from shattered lockers, the colour of the seating, but not people. She hadn't seen a single person, she realises, except the woman at the window.

Staring at her own face, reflected in the tiny mirror, she is sure of what she saw. The woman at the window, staring back at her, raising her hand not to touch the glass, but in a wave.

Her hotel is expensive. Gentile, beige modernity unfurls from the glass doors and potted palm trees to the counter, elevator and bar area. Her room is large, neat and bright. It overlooks a deserted pool area, empty deckchairs and tables beneath awnings, all surrounded by a high wall. Behind the ornate brickwork is the quayside and beyond that, the blue sea.

On the phone later that evening, her husband's voice seems unfamiliar – that of a person she once knew somewhere else, a long way away. 'Well thank God it wasn't your flight . . .'

She loses interest in what he is telling her. With the phone clamped against her shoulder, she flips through the pages of her diary. Her finger hovers over today's date and a scribble of altered plans. A chill passes through her. It was the plane she had been booked on before she had been persuaded to take an earlier flight – an opportunity to take some time for herself before the conference; a couple of days in the sun. But she is not used to leisure time, mistrustful of it. Her first day had been a tour of the island's unimpressive historical sites: monuments in sultry, cobbled squares and colonial ruins on the hills overlooking the marina. This, the second day, had been for shopping, until boredom and the clamour of the town had driven her to the beach.

Her husband is still talking. 'So what happened afterwards?'

'After what?'

'After the crash?'

'Look, I have to go. I still need to prepare for the presentation tomorrow.'

'Is everything alright, with you, I mean?'

'Yes, of course.'

'Okay. If you're sure?'

'Yes.'

'Okay. Bye. I love you.'

'Yes, of course,' she replies, and hangs up.

Caroline always requests a window seat in business class, the same part of the plane she had seen the woman at the window. It's impossible to tell for sure, but the woman may have been in her seat. It isn't difficult to look up a seating plan. Then she calls the emergency number that has been repeated at regular intervals on the news broadcasts.

'Is there a list of those on board?'

'A full list will be released when all families have been traced and contacted. Are you trying to locate a family member?'

'A friend.'

'What's their name?'

'She was in seat 5F.'

'And your friend's name please, ma'am?'

Later, showered, dressed, make-up re-applied, she goes

down to the bar. The chatter is inevitably all about the crash. There is nothing else to talk about.

Almost all of the patrons are men. Almost all are bragging, competing to be the one who was closest to the impact or most involved in the aftermath. A mingling of awe and jealousy is directed towards those who were closest to the action. She takes a gin and tonic to a table close to the bar, content to listen from a distance. The loud posturing of men is territory she is used to, and she finds the bullshit amusing.

A big man in a crumpled but expensive linen shirt turns to her from a nearby table. 'Did you see it?'

She hesitates, considering a lie.

'The crash,' he prompts, as though there could be any doubt.

'Yes.'

'Quite a thing, wasn't it?' He is well into his fifties, but his voice is deep, public-schoolish, overconfident in a way she once found attractive. 'I'm Hugh.'

They shake hands and she is drawn reluctantly into the dissection of the afternoon's events.

'I was on the beach when it happened,' he says, with a forced gravity that makes her want to laugh. She doesn't remember seeing him amongst the others, but to her surprise, she remembers very little about the afternoon, other than a meandering walk back to the hotel. Her memory of the event itself is like a video camera knocked out of focus and swinging about in a sweeping blur of imagery. Only occasionally is there a moment of clarity, a sharp detail: the men dragging boats down the beach; the roof of the aircraft peeling away; the woman at the window.

She lets him buy more gins while she listens to those around, all talking loudly, filled with a nervous need to explain, or to exorcise. The back-and-forth of the conversation rattles around her, although she barely hears it. When Hugh's attention falls back on her, she asks,

'You said you were along the beach from the bar, more or less as close as I was, maybe closer?'

'I guess so.'

'I have a question.'

'Shoot.'

'Did you . . . were you able to see anyone? On the plane, I mean, through the windows, or when it . . . Do you think you could see them well enough to recognise them?'

'No way. It was too far away and moving too fast.' Seeing her face, he adds, 'You didn't know someone who was aboard her, I hope?'

'No. Nothing like that . . .'

'Well, let me freshen your glass.'

She takes her drink out to the pool and the noise of the bar slips away. Staring into the surface of the water she can recall with absolute clarity how beautiful the plane looked in the moment before it broke up, with the sun bright on its fuselage, its wing tip about to touch the glistening membrane of the sea's shifting surface. The smooth carapace of the silver hull gave no indication of the events that must have been going on inside. These things would be spoken of later, at inquest hearings, in the testimony of the survivors. They will play the cockpit voice recordings full of indistinct shouts and electronic voice warnings: *Sink rate. Sink rate. Terrain. Terrain. Pull up. Pull up. Terrain. Terrain.*

For now, she imagines the panic of those last moments— a
slowed-down world – in which the woman in the window
seemed to see her, recognise her, and wave.

She is exhausted but can't sleep. There is a current running
through her, as though the percussion of the planes' disin-
tegration is still vibrating through her body. She lies on
her bed in the flickering light of the television. The only
channels in English are news channels. They are interested in only one subject. Other events: a coup in central
Africa; another right-wing American talking about
immigration; industrial disputes, are bumped down the
order and get only a brief mention at the end of each news
segment. Meanwhile, interview after interview ask the
same endlessly re-formulated questions: causes; terrorists;
pilot-error. Experts and technicians, less dramatic in their
demeanour than the salivating news-jockeys, suggest something more prosaic: there are six million working parts on
a modern airliner. Computer generated simulations of what
happened are intercut with footage captured on mobile
phones. Already, the plane, Sunworld Airlines Flight 458,
has become known by its call sign, Sunny 458.

On her laptop, she watches footage of the crash,
uploaded from phones. She replays them, freezing the
picture, searching for faces at the windows of the plane,
squinting at the blurred, low-res images of the shattering
fuselage. She pictures the plane as she had seen it in its
final moments, counts the windows, looks again at the
seating plan. She is certain – as certain as she can be – the
woman had been in her seat. On a clip of footage shot
from the beach, she sees herself. She freezes the picture.

In it, she is staring out, still holding her drink, smiling slightly as though she is watching a performance of some kind. Was that the moment when her eyes had met those of the woman at the window? What had it been like for her? Had she looked out, away from the panic unfurling around her, over the tropical sea, blue and still, the white sand of the beach, so close. Had she seen that little glimpse of paradise and imagined that things would be okay after all, because the plane was moving so slowly by then and the ground was so close, and a landing seemed possible after all as, somewhere in the noise behind her, the cabin crew shouted. *Brace. Brace. Heads down. Heads Down. Brace.*

When she finally sleeps, it is with the crash simulations quietly playing on the television. Electronic voices invade fleeting dreams before she falls deeper, away from the waking world. *Sink rate. Pull up. Sink rate.*

The morning is bright and breezy. She takes a cab. The taxi driver's eyes linger on her a moment too long. She slides across the seat, out of his line of sight.

'Town centre, please.'

'City.'

'Sorry?'

'City centre. We are a city.'

It doesn't feel like a city. She could walk across it in half an hour. The taxi is an extravagance.

She steps from one air-conditioned environment to another. The conference centre is glass-fronted, flags lining the pavement outside. In the foyer, service staff are dismantling tables. At the doors to the auditorium, an apologetic civil servant informs her that the conference has been cancelled. A number of the lead speakers were on Sunny 458. He smiles sympathetically and, on behalf of the Municipality and the Conference Centre, offers condolences for any colleagues she might have lost. Only when Caroline leaves does she realise that she has left her presentation materials in her hotel room.

She wanders through the central district. Most of the businesses are closed as a mark of respect and the main street is unnaturally quiet. On the quay she pauses, staring out across the sea, and thinks of all the distant cities full of people who are oblivious to the fate of Sunny 458. She recalls a bar – Singapore? Hong Kong? – Yes, maybe it was Hong Kong. Dark, no windows, but expensive. Catering for business men and women on stop over: people passing through. People still living in other time zones, gathering to drink Martinis at 10am local time. Frequent fliers, like her, never engaging with the locals, never having time to equalise to the pressure of their surroundings, getting drunk, dancing, enjoying liaisons that would not be mentioned in jet-lagged phone calls home. For those people, and billions of others, the news of a faraway plane crash was, at most, a passing moment of interest glimpsed on a TV screen while they made breakfast for the kids, queued for the bank, or sat in a bar drinking beer and eating pretzels.

At a newspaper stand, she pauses. The front pages show photographs of bodies laid out under sheets in a large room – a community hall or gymnasium. She can understand neither the headlines nor the captions, but she wonders if the photographs have been taken illicitly. They are invasive, as though the people in them have been filmed by a stalker as they slept.

The bodies are laid out in precise grids and each has two sets of numbers, one of which, she realises, are seat numbers. They have been arranged according to the seating plan – the matrix that decided who lived and who died. In the rigid arrangement of bodies there are gaps. Spaces left by the ones who refused their place amongst the orderly lines of their fellow passengers: the living. She thinks of the woman at the window – tries to work out where she would be. It is strange to think of her lying with the others, close enough that they could reach out and join hands with one another, as though the shrouded figures have chosen to lie together. These people, strangers in life, have been united in death: 'the victims', 'the dead', 'the passengers of Sunny 458'.

Caroline is thinking of this as she steps off the kerb and is nearly run over by a speeding Jeep. It dodges around her, horn blaring, as she jumps back. Shaking, on the pavement, she gathers herself, tucking her hair behind her ears and adjusting her sunglasses. Cautiously, she crosses the road and sets out towards the airport, even though it is hot and the terminal is two miles from town. Along the airport road, there is a line of cars, and when she reaches the single-storey terminal building, she finds a small crowd has gathered there.

Inside, people wander around dragging suitcases. The airport, they say, has been closed to non-essential traffic for twenty-four hours to allow investigators and emergency teams to fly in. The departures board confirms this. Back in London, the arrivals board will be showing incoming flights arriving from all over the world – Calgary, Basel, Dresden, Nice, Seoul, Jeddah, Oslo, Hamburg, Stavanger,

Sofia, Los Angeles – but not from here, not today. Boards
in other airports would announce cancelled departures.
Connecting flights would be missed, delayed. A minor
airline somewhere will ground its entire fleet of A320s
for routine maintenance. The share value of Sunworld
Airlines will tank, only to rally again later in the year
when fuel prices fall. A web of minor consequences and
electronic impulses fan out across the globe, dissipating,
becoming lost as they are swallowed by routine and
business-as-usual.

Caroline watches the people around her, wondering
who they are, why they're here, if they know how strange
this place is. She feels as though she has been cast adrift:
no longer here on business, nor is she here on vacation. She
is just here, moving through the day-to-day of island life
without a reason. To the world around her, she is irrelevant,
and for the first time in her life, Caroline feels invisible.
On her phone – switched off since the previous evening –
messages and emails are silently stacking up. At home, her
husband and daughter are going about their lives as though
she does not exist. They are as used to her absence as she is
used to theirs. She is due to fly back to them in two days,
what would have been the end of the conference, but she
feels the world slipping away from her and for a moment
she considers staying here, floating, half-way between two
continents. It is a fleeting thought. When a list, taped to a
white-board, tells her that her flight home is one of those
that will be rescheduled, she is filled with a sudden panic
– an urge to get home that goes beyond the usual yearning
for rest and the familiar.

Around the airport's only information desk, uniformed

personnel with clipboards are answering questions from anxious customers. It takes time to get to the front.

'I need to get home.'

'We're so sorry for any inconvenience caused by recent circumstances. We're making every effort to re-establish normal timetables. Please contact your airline directly to find out about flight alterations.'

Caroline begins to move away, but turns back to the desk clerk. 'Could you help me with something else? I know someone who was . . . She was in row five, seat F.'

'Their name please, ma'am,' says the clerk.

'Five F. Please check. It's very important.'

The clerk hesitates, but seems to yield, looking down at his monitor, scrolling through a list. She watches the pupils of his eyes as they move, searching rapidly down the screen in front of him. 'Five F was empty, ma'am.'

'Empty?'

'Yes, ma'am.'

'Do you have a list of passengers?'

'No, ma'am. If you give me your friends name . . .'

'I . . . I'm not sure.'

'Not sure?'

It is clear from the clerk's changing tone that he suspects her of something: perhaps of being a reporter, or just a ghoul.

'You should go please, ma'am. That information is for relatives only.'

His hand moves towards the phone, perhaps an empty threat, but she is already turning to leave.

She steps through the glass doors and into the sudden heat of the street outside. Standing beside the terminal, she watches the airstrip through the security fence. The angled shadows of airport buildings point across a neat strip of lawn to the tarmac and the sweeping geometry of the taxi-way.

On the apron, a plane is taxiing to a stand. The din of its turbines resonates through her body. Inside her, the vibration feels like fear. She feels a tremble running through her that matches the lowering pitch of the engines as they wind down.

Beyond the airport, across the scrub-land at the end of the runway, a small armada of boats and floating platforms have assembled at the crash site. The shoreline near the salvage operation is taped off, as preparations are made to raise the larger pieces of wreckage from the shallow water inside the reef. On the beach, the Minister for Commerce and Tourism, ashen faced, surveys the scene and addresses the press. Later he will attend the nearby resorts, shaking hands and listening to the complaints of outbound tourists whose flights have been delayed, and hotel managers who fear a downturn in visitor numbers. For a generation the island will be remembered as the scene of a tragedy. None of this matters to Caroline, or to the world across the ocean.

Out on the tarmac strip, the plane has come to a halt. Ground crew move towards it at a leisurely pace, conserving energy in the heat of the morning. Caroline watches the aircraft. It is a hundred feet closer to her than Sunny 458 had been when it hit the water, but from where she stands the windows are nothing more than small black smudges. Even at this shorter distance, she realises, she is unable to see through the dark bubbles of glass.

Caroline closes her eyes against the dust stirred up by

the jets, swirling in vortices in the hot breeze. The air is thick, and the smells of baked earth and engine fumes fill her nostrils. The dying whine of the aircraft engines and the heat of the day folding around her, squeezing the air from her lungs, carry her back to the beach and the sweet, sickly taste of a pineapple cocktail caught in her throat. She can see the rainbow hanging in the spray above the sinking wreckage and the woman in the window breaking apart with the fuselage, dissipating in the shimmer of heat and fumes, leaving no trace of herself.

Shooting Season

THE BUILDINGS OF the big house are hardly out of sight and I am already hot and thirsty. It's two miles to the bridge, maybe more, and the tractor is old and slow. The fiercest heat of summer has passed, but the estate still swelters in a lingering Indian summer and a haze hangs above the dirt road.

I pull off the track to allow one of the estate's four-by-fours to overtake me. I nod a greeting to the driver, Niall, but there is no response from the shadow behind the windscreen. Exhaust fumes and the smell of tyre-scuffed turf hang in the air as the Range Rover wallows over the gentle humps in the track. For a moment, before it disappears into the shallow valley, it seems to hover in the shimmering air.

Niall would usually stop and shoot the breeze for a while, but not today. His old university friends are here for the weekend; the first shooting party of the year. I follow on, the tractor rocking slowly beneath me as its wheels turn through dry potholes. Ahead of me the dust is still settling long after Niall's car has vanished from sight. Even here, a mile inland, the air is tinged with the smell of seaweed rotting along the distant tideline. Midges swarm in funnel-shaped clouds above depressions in the salt marsh where moisture has held on beneath the pallid crust.

The river, where I'm working, is little more than a glorified drainage ditch: a narrow watercourse cutting through the dunes to the sea beyond. I park the tractor beside the pile of new timber I dragged out here yesterday. I'm hot and sweating, and I'm tempted to slide into the water that runs dark and cold between high, steep banks. On a day like this it is simultaneously tempting and forbidding. Beyond the narrow bridge, the track follows the channel to the beach, dissolving into low, grass-tufted dunes. Three nearly identical four-by-fours are parked haphazardly there: Niall and his group playing guns and Land Rovers.

The river is spanned by thick wooden planking supported by two old, iron beams. Half of the timbers have been chewed away by tyres and the elements; the others are hard-cornered, regular, smelling of fresh wood preserver. Below, insects swarm in the cool air and skate across the still surface of the water. I drag new planks onto the bridge, pausing occasionally to stretch so that I can study the group in the distance. I half shut my eyes to see better against the light. She isn't there.

The party arrived in a steady trickle two days ago. She was the last to arrive and the only one to arrive alone, rolling down the drive to the big house in an elderly BMW. The first thing I noticed about her, even before she got out of the car, was her hair: a collapsed Mohawk dyed to resemble a flame. I should have ignored her, but I couldn't quite bring myself to look away. When she got out, kissing Niall on each cheek, I could see that a tattoo ran across her shoulder and down her arm to her elbow: the petals of deep-red roses intertwined with dark leaves. Niall was stand-offish, maybe annoyed that she was late, so I couldn't tell if they were together. She wasn't one of his usual girls. She looked like an arty type, or a bit of rough he'd picked up at some club or other.

She said her name was Lara – or maybe it had been Niall that had introduced her. She offered her hand, but before I could take it Niall said, 'That's just Wayne. He's one of our groundsmen. He'll be around to help out over the weekend.' Her hand fell back to her side and she moved instead to take her bag from the back of the car. 'Wayne can bring that in for you. Come on, we're all going down to the summer house for drinks.' Without looking back, he added, 'Thank you, Wayne.'

She hovered at the edge of my vision for the rest of the long, still afternoon. From where I was working, at the perimeter of the garden, I watched them. The other girls, all blandly good looking, well dressed, bored, were sticking to the terrace and each other. Lara walked around the gardens with the boys. She strolled at the back of the group, but they seemed to be pushed along by an unseen wave, constantly looking back, competing for attention.

I tried again to work out if she was with Niall, but there were no obvious signs either way. Perhaps she was a spare. That would explain her distance from the other girls: a threat.

As I work, crouched on the bridge, sweat drips from me, soaking into the parched fibres of the wood. The bolts securing the planks have rusted into chestnut-brown clots, but the grinder cuts easily through the old metal and burns into the timber. The smell of scorched metal will cling to me for the rest of the day.

Lara arrives unexpectedly, walking down the track towards me. She is not alone. With her is Lucas, Niall's twelve-year-old brother, wearing a rugby shirt that he has long outgrown, broad blue and white stripes stretched tight around his tubby body.

I carry on wrenching out the old timbers, my head down, until I can hear the sound of her feet nearby on the path. I release the length of rotten timber I'm prizing loose and look up, smiling. Lucas, watchful, hangs back and climbs up into the seat of the tractor as she walks onto the bridge.

I point at the loosened planks. 'Watch your step.'

'My car broke down. Do you think you could have a look at it for me, or give it a tow? I tried phoning Niall, but there's no signal.'

She talks like the others, but I can see the moment's hesitancy before each action, uncertain of the correct etiquette. It's easy to spot the ones who weren't born to it.

I nod, trying not to let it feel too significant that it is me she has turned to for help. We make polite conversation for a while and I watch the sweat beading on her skin and track the distortion of the flowers on her shoulder as she reaches up to shield her eyes from the sun.

'Are you coming shooting?' she asks, not quite looking at me. It's a strange question; she knows I'm not one of the guests.

'No. I stay out of the way.' She looks a bit alternative, an eco-warrior type, so I try my luck: 'I don't hold with hunting. Cruel.'

'Oh.'

'You don't look very keen yourself.'

'I don't care. They're only fucking birds. Anyway, I don't think Niall would know a duck if it flew out of his arse.'

'The seagulls must be terrified.'

She smiles before turning to look down the track towards the rest of the party.

'How do you know Niall?' I don't mean it to sound as loaded as it does, too urgent in the asking. 'I mean, how long have you been—' I hesitate, '—friends?'

'Not long.' To my relief, she smiles. 'I've got to go and join the others. I'm sure I'll see you around. I'll be here for a couple of days. My car's over there.' She points down the track in the direction of the big house as she walks away. 'I left the keys in it.'

'I'll finish this and I'll bring the tractor down.'

'Thanks. It's sweet of you.'

Down the track, she hesitates, looking back for a moment before walking on.

Leaning on the edge of the bridge I start to grind out another bolt, watching her reflection in the glassy water as she walks away, but her image is shattered by the impact of a rock. I had forgotten Lucas. Behind me he is balancing on one of the bridge beams, holding stones that he's prized from the bank, each as smooth and dark as the water. He drops them one at a time. Each disappears with a baritone splosh. When the last one has gone, he comes closer and stands with his hands on his hips in front of me.

'Hello, Lucas. I thought I could smell something.'

'She's my brother's girlfriend.'

'Is she?'

'Yes. I'm just telling you so you know.'

'Sounds like you've been keeping an eye on her.'

'She wouldn't be interested in you.'

'Is that right?'

'What were you talking to her about?'

'None of your business, you little maggot.'

'I really don't think she'd like you very much. You're not her type. We're good friends you see, so I think she would have told me.'

'Go away, Lucas. I'm busy.'

'You shouldn't talk to me like that. If Father found out he might let you go.'

'Why don't you go and tell Niall all about it?'

Lucas climbs back into the seat of the tractor.

'Get off there, Lucas!'

'It belongs to Father, not you,' he says, climbing down and scuttling towards the bridge.

I throw the tools into my bag and hang it behind the tractor seat. When I heave myself up and go to start the engine the key has gone. I punch the steel rim of the steering wheel and Lucas's name escapes from me like a hissed release of pressure. I swing round in the seat to see him standing on the edge of the bridge, grinning, his arm stretched over the water, the tractor key clutched in his chubby fingers.

'Give me that key, Lucas, or I'll give you such a fucking leathering!'

I climb down, and when I turn back towards the bridge, Lucas has gone. I shout his name and scan the long grass on the riverbank. There is only one place he can be. By the time I am peering down into the water beneath the bridge, only a slowly dispersing ring of foam marks the spot where the surface was disrupted. There had been no sound, as though the heat of the day made the water too lazy to leap back from the impact or waste energy sending waves to slap against the banks. I wait, expecting Lucas to burst back up, spluttering into the sunshine, but there is no movement. The world is quiet.

I rip at the laces of my heavy work-boots, kicking them off, and shout down the track to the others. They see me waving and grabbing at my boots. They wave back, laughing. I shout again, but the words seem out of place in the sapping stillness of the morning. My voice is hushed by the air, as though the sound won't carry through its thick warmth.

I drop from the bridge into the river, unprepared for the sudden cold. It sucks the air from my lungs and I gulp in a throatful, rising quickly back to the surface. I am momentarily blinded by the sun and by the brackish water pouring across my eyes. Lunging into the centre of the waterway, I feel the water's mass pressing against me as I swing my arms around, searching. The river is barely moving; the boy can't have been pulled far.

I duck under the water, fingers stretching into the darkness beneath the bridge. A single beam of light shines through a gap in the planks above me, illuminating a column of water clouded by a storm of silt and debris stirred up by my flailing search. In this faint glow the boy emerges, hanging in the water as though he has congealed out of river sludge.

My hands collide with his torso, soft and heavy, and I grab for a slippery arm that slides from my grasp as the buoyancy of the air in my lungs forces me to the surface. Diving beneath the water again, I breathe out as I sink and manage to grab the boy's hair, dragging him up towards the bank. It is high and sheer. I drag Lucas further along the gully to a place where the bank is shallow enough to lift him out. I heave the kid onto my shoulder, but even here, where the bank is lowest, his dead weight defeats me.

When my breath returns I begin to shout again. My voice echoes against the banks and seems impossibly loud. When the others arrive at the bridge their laughter stops so abruptly that it makes me want to laugh back at them. They reach down, dragging the boy from my shoulders, struggling to get a grip on his wet skin as his shirt peels away.

On the riverbank, Lara is nowhere in sight, neither is Niall. Someone goes to look for them while another takes one of the Land Rovers back to the house to phone for help. The others crouch nearby, staring at their useless phones, or wait further along the track, as if to deny their involvement.

The boy's lips are blue. In the warming sun, his chest rises and falls as I blow air into him. It is strange how easy it is to fill the lungs of another human being, to watch their cheeks bulge and chest expand with the effort of your own breathing. As I look down at him, I wonder what his older brother is doing with Lara, down there in the dunes.

I pause, needing air myself, silty water still dripping from my hair, stinging my eyes and blurring the brightness of the day that is spinning around me. I sit astride the inert child, pumping his chest. If the boy dies the shooting party will be over. She will go and she will not return.

Later, they will say later how desperately I fought to save him.

My skin tightens as the sun dries me. The tiny grains of stone in the gravel beneath the boy's head catch the light and I see a black beetle tumbling through the flattened grass beside us. I picture Lara walking back along the track, pausing to look at the sun-baked landscape, maybe hearing the distant shouts from the riverbank and mistaking them for the cries of gulls. I think about how, in the glare of the sun, the deep-red ink of the roses curling softly down the skin of her shoulder had looked almost black. I watch Lucas's chest for any sign of independent movement. As I bend to blow air into his lungs again, I look out along the river channel, beyond the dunes, to the distance where the sea is a shimmering strip of blue.

Downstream the Water Darkens

T HERE ARE ONLY a few days before we have to go home. Summer is nearly over, a flash of brilliant blue and green that came and went, like the dragonflies near the water's edge.

Kristin and I are on the riverbank at the furthest corner of the farm. The fields end at a wall of hawthorn tangled with curls of ancient barbed-wire; an impenetrable barrier that stretches all the way to the distant road. There is nothing here, just a few yards of scrubby field and an old feeding trough surrounded by thistles; a forgotten corner where the adults never come.

We stand together on the shingle at the edge of The Pool – a broad, still section of the river formed in the sweep of a bend. Beyond the open fields of the farm, the river curves out of sight between high banks topped with densely planted trees. They grow so close together that it's impossible to see more than a few feet beyond the boundary of the plantation. Here, at the edge of the wood, the water is a deep brown and cold.

She's laughing at me – 'You're a liar. You'll just hide

somewhere and say you went.' She's trying to make out she isn't afraid to go, but she's already walking back towards the house, watching me over her shoulder.

I shout after her, 'I'll take pictures. Proof.' I have a camera of my own. It's small enough to carry in my pocket or on a string around my neck; an oblong of black plastic with a clip to attach flash cubes.

Ahead of me, the top of the bank is fenced off. The only way to follow the river is to wade through the shallows at the edge of The Pool. But that is where the pike lives. A monster, at least six feet long. I've never seen this pike – or any other – but I've listened to the stories about it. I've heard anglers describe it to the farmer; the monstrous size of it, it's immense age and cunning, lying in wait, perfectly still in the depths of The Pool. It has been caught more than once and hauled onto the riverbank before fighting its way free and plunging back into the dark, into legend, before a camera shutter could click.

I look downstream, where none of us have been, where the river disappears into the land beyond. I touch the knife in my pocket for reassurance, tracing the detail of the plastic grip and the single folding blade of cheap steel. It feels more dangerous because it was stolen.

I know I can't back out, not after what happened at the village. As I take my first steps into the water, I shout, 'You better not say anything to the others.' But Kristin is already out of range. Secretly, I hope she will tell Alice and Sam. I know they'll be impressed. But I'll be in trouble if my aunt and uncle find out – and worse trouble if they tell my father. Every time I speak to him on the phone, he reminds me how good it is of them to take me on holiday, even though I'd rather stay at home with him. I don't feel comfortable with them. They're posh. You can tell by their car, and the way they call the Prime Minister 'Mrs Thatcher' when they're talking about the news. In our house she's just 'Thatcher', especially since Dad lost his job.

This is the second summer that I've been sent on holiday with my cousins, but it's the first time Kristin, Alice's best friend, has come. At first there was a split: two teams – boys and girls. The unspoken plan had been for me to play with Sam and leave the girls to themselves, but Sam is only nine and I was bored, then Alice got ill so Kristin grew bored too. Alice and Sam are the sort of kids who are always catching colds or crying because they're afraid of being stung by a wasp.

I wade out slowly. Under the high bank, the surface of the water is like black glass. I begin to cross The Pool staying close to the side, my hand searching for projecting roots to hold onto. I can feel the pike watching me. I sense it, down there in the dark. I want to go faster, but the thin rubber soles of my shoes don't offer much protection against the stones of the riverbed, and the aching cold makes it hurt more. I don't show the pain in case Kristin is still watching. The water is half way up my thighs now, and here, away from the main channel, the only ripples come from my churning strides that grow slower as the depth increases. In the gloom under the trees, the water seems heavier, as though gravity is stronger here. Staring at the glassy surface, watching for any signs of movement, I suddenly become aware of my own reflection. I am surprised how serious I look.

I reach the pebble beach beyond The Pool. I am out of

sight of the farm now; out of sight of Kristin, of anyone. I am alone. At the farmhouse it will be as though I don't exist. If I slip and smash my skull on the slippery rocks, I would die and nobody would be there to see it. But that won't happen; I'm a careful climber and a good swimmer. If I wanted to, I could keep going, run away, and only Kristin would know. Would she come looking for me?

I climb across a sloping face of rock. I have entered another world. The river is different here. It is difficult to imagine that this is the same water that shimmered across the sun-warmed shallows near the house, where we had played all summer. Along its banks there are no meadows or signs of human habitation; the quiet water is watched over only by the creatures living in the dark of the pine woods, where the ground is soft with deep drifts of needles and the gloom sucks in every sound and keeps it. Not a single bird crosses the stripe of sky that follows the river's path through the woodland. Even the insects that buzz around the bright pools upstream seem to shun the water here. The hum and clatter of summer's wings has gone, and the water has forgotten how to sparkle or how to murmur as it passes. Only fallen leaves floating along the river's dark centre betray any movement.

From the start of the holiday, I was mesmerised by Kristin; a little overwhelmed by her self-confidence, and fascinated by the way her hair fell across her eyes and the coldness of the goose-bumped skin on her arms as the four of us walked back to the house shivering after playing in the river. When I followed her to the village, it was to make sure she was okay. She'd gone alone and I was worried.

Alice was in bed and Sam had gone bird-watching with his father. I found her easily enough. The village is tiny: a shop with a petrol pump outside; a village hall made from corrugated steel, and a few cottages. We sat on the wall beside the shop and ate the sweets she'd bought until a couple of local kids, a boy and a girl, arrived. They were older than us, fourteen or fifteen, and tough looking. We watched them turn down a narrow track that led behind the scatter of buildings.

Kristin jumped down, excited. 'Come on, let's spy on them.'

I sensed trouble and wanted to go back. But she was fearless.

The two kids went around the back of one of the sheds. We snuck along the edge of the track and crawled through long damp grass behind a tumbledown wall. By the time we poked our heads around the edge of a missing section of masonry, they were kissing. I started to snigger. Kristin didn't; she was suddenly serious, as though she was watching something important, not a couple of village kids feeling each other up. I started to pay attention too. Lying crushed together in the lee of the wall, I noticed for the first time the smell of Kristin's skin and the heat of her body beside me. Our limbs were touching, and it felt different to when we played in the river, when our skin was ice cold and our fingers numb. I moved away from her, embarrassed, but she was paying no attention to me. Her eyes were glued to the gap in the wall.

I took out my camera, tilted its lens towards Kristin and pressed the shutter. She pretended to be annoyed, as she did every time I photographed her. She preferred to strike a pose, like one of her favourite actresses. I wound the film on and we both turned our attention back to the village kids.

They didn't see us at first. I'd just taken their picture when the boy turned and looked straight at me. We scrambled to our feet and ran for it. He was much faster than me. I didn't even make it as far as the road. He grabbed me by the neck, long fingers pressing like pincers. He ignored Kristin. She stood a short distance away, unsure what to do. She didn't leave, but she was keeping her distance.

'What are you doin', you fuckin' little pervy?'

I said nothing.

'Spying on us, were you?' The girl joined him and they pushed me back behind the sheds. Up close, they seemed much bigger. Kristin stood on the track nearby, passive and safely out of range. The boy pushed me against the wall and took something out of his pocket. A penknife. 'You stay there, pervy.'

I couldn't speak, so I stood with my hands clamped to my side, palms sweating. He unfolded the blade of the knife and they took it in turns to throw it at the shed wall, close to where I stood. I was afraid I'd look like a coward if I ran. Afraid of what he would do if he caught me again. I tried to remain still, to look unafraid, but each time the knife struck the wood beside me, I jumped involuntarily. Sometimes it stuck, sometimes it bounced off.

It was Kristin who spoke. Without a hint of fear in her voice, she said; 'If you don't let him go, I'm going to call the police.'

The girl replied, 'If you try it, I'm gonna knock your teeth in. He your boyfriend, is he?'

'No. No way.' At that moment I hated her almost as

much as I hated them. The boy turned back to me and
came in close. He held the knife up to my face.

'I see you round here again, right, an' I'll cut your balls
off.'

He shook me slowly by the neck, almost playing. Behind
him, the girl sniggered as he dropped me and slapped me
hard on the side of the head. They strolled off towards the
main road at the head of the valley. I started walking in the
other direction, back towards the farm, but Kristin stayed
where she was and watched them go. She stared until they
were out of sight.

'What you so interested in those hedge-monkeys for?'

Finally, she turned around and snapped, 'You ruin
everything.'

I wasn't sure what it was I had ruined. 'It was you that
wanted to spy on them.'

'You're such a coward. Why didn't you fight him?' She
stared, indignant. 'Stop following me around.'

She should never have said that, not after I went to the
village to find her, but she had said it. I was ashamed that
I hadn't fought back, and that she had seen my failure. I
couldn't walk back with her, so I turned round and headed
back to the petrol station.

I wanted more than anything to go home, but I knew it
was impossible. Instead, I decided to call my dad from the
phone box in the centre of the village. It was cleaner than
the ones where we lived, and it still had its windows. There
was even a directory on a shelf. I dropped a ten-pence coin
into the slot and dialled. It seemed strange to think that
150 miles away, the phone in our hallway was ringing. I
could feel the distance, the miles of wire slung between

poles, stretching across the country to the one place in the world I knew. I half expected some other version of myself to answer, but it was Dad who picked it up, sounding tired.

'Hello, yes?'

'Dad?'

'Yeah?'

'It's me.'

'What's wrong?'

'Nothing. Just wanted to say hello.'

'Okay.' I could hear him doing something else while we were talking. A metallic clatter. He could have been working, or it could have been the lid of his tobacco tin. There was a long pause before he asked, 'How are your cousins?'

'They're okay.'

'Okay then.'

'I'm taking pictures. Like we said. So you can see what it's like.'

'Good.'

'Okay.' I tried desperately to think of something I could tell him. Something I had done. Something that would impress him. But what Kristin had said was true.

'See you in a few days,' he said.

'Okay.'

'Bye.'

'Dad?' But he'd gone.

I hung up the receiver, pushed the door of the phone box open, and crossed the road to the petrol station. Inside, amongst the groceries and hardware hanging from racks, was a display board of penknives. I touched one lightly with my fingertips.

The shopkeeper was a fat man with grey hair and a grey coat. At that moment he was looking the other way, out of breath with the effort of moving some boxes along the floor with his foot. I slipped the knife into my pocket, then went to the counter and chose some sweets so he wouldn't be suspicious. I pushed down my fear as I waited for him to serve me.

'Will there be anything else?' He knew. I felt the colour draining from my face. But he just smiled. 'That everything, is it?'

I nodded and put the money for the sweets on the counter wordlessly. I felt the knife in my pocket as I put my change away. Outside, all I could think of was the others' faces when I showed them my new weapon.

When I got back to the farm, Kristin was where I expected: with Alice, lying on a rug in the meadow. She was reading a magazine, laughing in the fake way she does when she tries to sound like somebody off the telly. As I got nearer, I realised they were talking about the boy from the village. When they saw me, they shut up. I pretended I hadn't heard.

I took the knife out to show them, then started throwing it at a nearby bank of earth so that its blade stuck into the soft, dry turf. I longed for Kristin to ask for a go throwing it. If Alice hadn't been there she would have. By the time I'd had a few practice throws, Sam had arrived. I told him it was a hunting knife and let him have a go.

'Where did you get it?' Alice asked. 'You don't have enough money.'

'I took it. From the shop.'

'You idiot,' Kristin said.

The flicker of excitement that had briefly appeared on Alice's face vanished. 'Yes, you idiot. What if you'd been caught?' She made Sam stop playing with it.

Bruised, I wandered away from them, along the river-bank. There was no breeze and the sun's heat was gathering in the hollows of the meadow. I lay on my stomach looking at grass stalks in the water, silver bubbles clinging to them like mercury, defying the current. Turning my head, I stared along the surface of the river, eyes screwed up against the dazzling white of the glare from the water as it burst over stones. I looked past the rapids to the edge of the farm, where the trees almost touched above the river, sending it into a gloomy, green darkness.

That was when I decided on my expedition. The next morning, early, while the others were still making break-fast, I would follow the river as far as I could go. I would have something to tell Dad. He'd be angry at first that I'd gone off alone, but then he'd understand. Later, he'd be glad that I'd done it – maybe even proud of me. I'd tell only Kristin where I was going; I'd whisper it to her that evening, a secret; something she couldn't resist.

In the sunless gloom, I feel cold. The skin on my bare legs and arms prickles. Looking at the dark avenues between the trees, I begin to wonder how far I should go; how far do I need to go? How far downstream would the pike come? I touch the knife in my pocket before moving on and I feel something I have not experienced before: the rush of being somewhere, alone. The shadows connect with something inside me: a growing need for secrecy; a feeling of being on the edge of something that I almost understand.

I press on, picking my way across an expanse of moss-covered rocks, following the boulders for a long way until, at last, the river begins to change again. Emerging from the gloom, it is still surrounded by trees, but they are thinner and the banks are lower and further apart. Through the scattered copses I can see the land rolling towards places I have never been. Distant hills and towns that remind me the world is bigger than I'd thought. The water here seems alive again and has its voice back. I stop to splash my face. The river carries the earthy smell of distant territories: the headwaters from the moorland above the farm, and the streams flowing there, peaty, never warm, even on the hottest day. My reflection is almost unrecognisable in the shimmering surface. Staring into the moving water dizzies me for a moment. As I straighten, I see, on the far side of the river, something bright, electric blue, like the flash of a ray gun. The object, whatever it is, is as alien here as me and I am immediately drawn to it.

The river is broad and shallow and being back in the strong, clear light of the sun has made me bold again. I begin to wade across the riffle, but it is deeper than I thought and the current faster. The resistance against my legs makes me feel I'm barely moving. As I push towards the other side, each stride is harder and harder. I pass the point of no return, the far bank is closer now and I have to hold my camera up to keep it out of the water. What I had thought to be a shallow stretch has turned out to be more formidable. If the others had been here, I would front it out, wade on and laugh at them. But alone, with only the noise of the water to break the silence, it's different.

As I pause, looking for an easier path, I see something

in the water; near the far bank, beneath overhanging trees, something breaking the surface. The long arc of a fish's back. A massive fish. A predator. The pike is here. Perhaps it has been with me all the time, watching from the deep pools, waiting for its chance. My legs shake with the effort of pushing onwards. Every piece of weed that brushes my leg has become something else now: the touch of a spiny tail or the taunting graze of a passing fin. But even in my need to escape, part of me is hoping I'll be the first to photograph the monstrous pike.

I lunge out of the water onto the rocks, legs almost buckling beneath me. As soon as I sense safety, I aim my camera down towards the place I saw the monster lurking. I slither and crawl across the rocks for a clear shot. My finger is poised on the shutter release, but all I find is the tip of a branch dipping into the water, tugged by the current, sending out a curling wave of silver.

I sit for a moment. After the ice cold, the rocks are wonderfully warm. I look back to where I came from. The far bank seems different from here. Like seeing an old photograph and not quite being able to remember where you took it.

I get my breath back and turn to find the object that drew me to this side of the river. Now that I'm closer, I see it's just an old fertilizer bag, caught under a branch in the shallows. But there is something inside it. The glistening plastic bulges, fat with something. It's partly weighted down in the water, but bobs against the spur of rock that halted its journey downstream. I have to find out what's inside. Whatever it is, someone has thought to bind it thoroughly; it's tied tight shut. But I have the knife, so the bailing twine wound around the neck of the bag feels more like an invitation than a deterrent.

I think of the others, upstream. They'll be sunbathing or making up some stupid game. But I have been further, seen more. In the bag is something they don't have, a secret that will belong only to me.

The bag is heavy. I drag it, with effort, up the bank. Despite being tied up, the bag has taken on water and whatever is inside sloshes around as I drag it. I take out my knife. Its cheap blade is barely up to the task of hacking through the twine. I pull the blade upwards, sawing until the fibres give with a snap and I fall back as the contents of the bag pour out in a stinking flood of blood red, washing across my feet, carrying with it the broken bones and battered pieces of the thing inside.

I take out my camera.

Meadowlands

THE TREETOPS ARE stirring against a milky sky. The hiss rises to a roar as the wind builds, rolling in waves through the highest boughs, but all that noise and motion is far above my head. Down here on the sodden ground the air is still and thick and I feel as though I am underwater.

Meadowlands is changing. The spruce are being replaced acre by acre, replanted with other trees. People dislike the conifers. They are foreign invaders. Their uniformity and the darkness beneath their closed ranks make them easy to hate, but I enjoy the silence they bring; the way their thick bed of needles and oily wood suck noise out of the air. They keep secrets. In the densest parts of the plantation, you can't see more than a few metres. It's easy to lose your way in there, and people do. Walkers, coming down off the hills, trying to take a short cut, get confused by the false perspectives in the avenues between the trees, made worse with having no horizon to navigate by. I hear them sometimes, crashing through the wood. Occasionally I find the prints of walking boots weaving through the plantation.

Out here, on the edge of the estate, the genteel parkland at its centre is a distant fantasy. You can scream all you want, nobody will come. I know this for a fact. When I first started working here, felling the spruce, I dropped a tree in the wrong direction and, before I could jump clear, it caught me across the ankle. I shouted for a long time before I realised just how alone I was. I limped back to the road where, at last, I caught a phone signal. Doyle came for me in the Land Rover. I had no one else to call.

'I've broken my ankle. It's fucked. Don't touch it.'

As usual, Doyle was unimpressed and reluctant to interrupt his cigarette. He made no attempt to touch it until we got back to the caravan we shared. He helped me in and dropped me on my bed. I picked at my laces while he rolled another cigarette. When he was ready, he said, 'I need to see it. Hold still.'

Holding his unlit cigarette between thin, pale lips, he set about taking off my boot. I couldn't look. It hurt a lot, and finally he lost patience with my squirming and yanked the boot clear. Horror washed over his face.

'Jesus, lad. It's a fucking mess. They'll never be able to save that. I'm going for an ambulance. Your tree-felling days are over, son. Best you don't look.' He laid a tea towel gently across my foot so I wouldn't have to see the extent of my injuries. A spot of blood began to seep through the pattern. I tried to hold back tears as he dashed out of the caravan sobbing. It was only after he'd been outside for a while that I realised he was laughing.

'It's not funny. You fucking old bastard, Doyle.'

'Ah, you soft wee prick. It's a sprain. A couple of aspirin and a day sitting on your backside and you'll be fine. Here.

Let me see. Can you move your toes? You're fine. I told you. Get a bag of peas on it.'

We didn't have any peas, so I used a four-pack of lagers from the fridge.

Nobody but me comes out to the fringes of the plantation, not even the other estate workers. The owners probably don't even know these places exist. The trees have never been properly managed and they are cramped and raggedy. But, among the conifers are bright clearings where trees have fallen and sudden islands of life have sprung up in the middle of a dark-green ocean. There is a network of overgrown tracks cut by forestry trucks decades ago, humid and humming with insects. They lead nowhere. Keep following them and they peter out. By the time you reach the deer-fencing at the edge of the moor, the paths have fanned out into sheep trails that climb through the heather to the steep slopes beyond the estate.

I prefer to work alone. That usually means following the main work party, clearing undergrowth and stacking logs. I love the smell of fresh-cut timber and the fumes from the chainsaw mingling with the smell of my own body and the heavy, damp wool of my work jacket. But not every day can be a winner; this week I'm working with Doyle. The underwater stillness of my secret clearings will have to wait.

I head back towards the middle of the estate. At this time of the morning, there won't be another soul on the miles of track that criss-cross the woodland. Later, the other men will be out working, and hill walkers will arrive, but even around the loch, at the centre of the glen's wide belly, there are places nobody goes and the only sound is the water lapping quietly at its muddy banks.

I meet Doyle on the road. He's in the old Land Rover, driving up to meet me.

'How come you're up so early, young man? You shit the bed?'

'Just thought I'd go for a walk before work.'

'Glad you're feeling so energetic. Time to graft.'

I get in and he guns the engine. The failing drive-shaft clatters as the Landy labours its way along the steep, gravel track. It's a long, slow drive across the glen. We are repairing an access track beyond the loch. There are always road repairs to be done here. The erosion is constant. A slow peeling away of the surface by the burns that drain the uplands. The peat and forest stain the water dark red-brown as it gathers into broader arteries feeding the loch. The water is held back by an earth dam. The shallows around it are choked with silt and broad-leafed grasses, and the trees that grow along the banks are lank, reluctant, as though, instead of sustaining them, the water is drawing life from them.

The road skirts the loch closely, but the undergrowth is so dense, so entangled with the lower branches, that the water isn't visible. Still, I find myself staring into the darkness beneath the trees, unable to look away, straining for a glimpse. As we pass the end of the loch's access road, I notice fresh tyre tracks. Someone must have been down to the water. A cold wave of nausea washes through my guts.

'See that! Someone's been down there.' I try to sound disinterested – only curious – but my voice is shaking.

'Aye. They're building a new drain.'

'A drain?'

'Aye. For the water levels.'

I try not to let him sense my anxiety. 'When? Which part of the loch? When?'

'Soon. I don't know.' He looks at me, maybe suspicious, it's hard to tell with Doyle.

'When though? You must have heard something.'

'What the fuck does it matter? What's up with you? You been smoking your funny cigarettes again?'

I feel sick. If someone is poking around by the loch, they'll find her, and when they do, they'll ask around town and someone will tell them what happened at Killian's, and they'll come straight to me.

I'm still shaking when Doyle stops the truck and we start to unload our tools. As I'm throwing our picks and shovels onto the roadside, something on the track attracts my attention: a tiny orb of gloss black. It is the eye of a young bird lying motionless between furrows of churned mud.

'Injured,' Doyle grunts.

I approach it slowly, cupping my hands around it. It barely moves until I lift it free of the mud. Injured though it is, I feel it pressing outwards against my palms, a warm fluttering, not just of its wings, but its whole body; a heartbeat, a tremble and an attempt at flight all joined in a single desperate rhythm. The tiny, black eye remains fixed on me as I place it on the turf bank beside the road and pile some leaves around it for protection.

Doyle is watching me with his piano-wire smile fixed. I feel myself blush. He thinks I'm soft, so I stand up and stamp on it, hard. Through the heavy sole of my boot the crunch is barely noticeable.

Doyle shakes his head. 'What the fuck did you do that for?'

'It'd die anyway.'

'If you say so, nurse.'

The physicality of digging calms me. I concentrate on the cutting of the ground with the spade and the weight of the wet earth as I lift it from the trench we're creating, but my mind is racing. If the girl wasn't naked, they'd just think it was an accident . . . maybe.

But, even after what happened in town, there had to be other suspects in the frame. As we work, I tell Doyle about the townies who come to the car park on a Saturday night when the walkers have all gone home. 'They drive up here to smoke gear and fuck.'

One weekend, not long ago, I'd watched from a hiding place in the trees as two boys persuaded a girl to raise her skirt and show her arse. They gave her booze and got her to take her knickers off. I didn't want to see anymore so I threw the empty vodka bottle I'd been drinking from. It smashed against a tree and all three of them froze like animals, then ran for it, back to their car.

'There's no telling what would have happened if I hadn't been there,' I tell Doyle.

'What. The. Fuck. Are. You. On. A-bout?' He says each syllable slowly as though I'm a retard or something.

The caravan smells of butane and the dust burning on the bars of the electric fire. Doyle has the big bedroom, which we refer to as 'the master suite'. The second bedroom, just big enough for a bunk bed, stinks, so I sleep on the floor of the lounge area, using the sofa cushions for a mattress. At first I used to clear my makeshift bed away every morning, but not anymore. Occasional we get a temp worker staying here, but neither of us likes having a guest and they never stay long. Not everyone can deal with Doyle.

After dinner, I drink too much. There is nothing else to do except listen to Doyle swearing at the portable TV while he exchanges texts with one of the other estate workers. Most nights, the other men take the Landy into town.

'Right, come on, laddy. Get your Old Spice on, we're away.'

'I'm not going.'

They'll only end up drinking at Killian's place again, and after what happened last time, it's better I keep my head down. Besides, I'm tired from digging and anaesthetised by the beer.

'Suit yerself.'

He slams the door behind him and I hear his heavy booted feet trudging down the lane. I turn down the volume on the telly and open the windows. The beginnings of a headache are soothed by the damp gloom. I have a ciggie and listen to the soft hiss of rain on the ferns and grass that grow a metre high all around the 'van.

I smoke until the beer wears off, then sleep for a bit. When Doyle comes back from town, he's brought me two and a half litres of Frosty Jack cider in a blue plastic bottle. He's always good like that, Doyle. The time I fucked up my ankle, he made me sandwiches so I wouldn't have to get off the bed, and he left me some beers and fags. He didn't even make me pay him back.

He's no angel though. He has a temper when he drinks. And he's been inside. He told me once, when he was pissed. 'That's why I couldn't get a proper job and why I'm livin' in this dump with a dick like you.' I don't think he even remembers now that he told me.

Obviously, I asked what he'd done and how long he was in for, but he wouldn't tell me. Speaking into his near-ly-empty beer can between gulps, all he said was, 'I was in for long enough to find out you don't ask what people did. I paid my dues.'

I knew not to push Doyle, even when he was in a good mood, but I was feeling cocky. 'Were you guilty? Did you do it?'

'It doesn't matter. Once those bastards have got you in their sights, they don't care who they pin it on.'

That was all I got out of him. He was getting arsey, so I backed off.

That conversation was a while back now, but as I remember it, I feel a ray of hope for the first time in days. When they find her, they'll check the records of everyone on the estate. Surely, they must. And like he said, they'll just look for someone to pin it on. I take a long swig of beer. 'Cheers, Doyle.'

For three days I dig nervously in the sun. On our day off, it rains. Nobody fancies going to town. Not until later anyway. The humidity brings the midges out and the air in the caravan is choked with the smell of burning mosquito coils. The stinking smoke is probably poisoning us both, but neither of us wants to be eaten alive.

If nobody is heading into town, there is nothing to do but drink and smoke. Whenever Doyle drinks there's the usual bullshit to deal with. One of the other grunts on the estate has been promoted – Pavel, a polish guy – and Doyle is fuming about it. I can't get the full story, and if I asked him it would make him worse.

'All these Poles and shite, takin' all the fuckin' jobs. I should be doin' that job. White niggers, that's what they are, I'm tellin' you.'

I figured out ages ago that when he's like this – pissed and worked up – it doesn't go well if you take him on. I grunt, as I usually do, and he takes it as a sign of agreement. In my mind I pretend I'd told him to fuck off. It's not like I give a shit, but he keeps on and on.

'For fuck's sake, Doyle. If you're so much better than him, how come he got the job.'

'Coz he's a fucking foreigner and we've all got to be politically bloody correct. And he's a fuckin' arse kisser.'

'Maybe you should pucker up, too.'

'What do you know? How old are you? You're fucking twelve or somethin'. This your first job? Second? You know nothing.'

'Aye and I bet I get a promotion before you do.'

'Don't you get smart with me, you little bastard.'

'I can't stand this place. How come I've got to share this shit-box with you?'

'You can fuck off and sleep in the woods anytime you want to. You think I like having you under my fucking feet all the time.'

He is spitting angry. A piece of baked bean flies from his mouth and lands in his drink. It stops him, as though he's embarrassed or he's waiting to see if I've noticed. He stares at me for a moment, and I stare back, holding his gaze for a long time. Doyle can be pretty scary when he's like this, and I come close to shitting myself. When he jumps up, I come even closer, but he just storms into his bedroom, still swearing to himself, and shuts the door. Through the flimsy wall I hear, 'You need a slap. Teach you some fucking manners.'

I get up and slam my plate down on the draining board. With a chipboard wall between us, I feel braver. Standing in the caravan door with my hand on the latch, I shout, 'Fuck off, you old bastard,' and duck out. As I stride up the track, the door is flung open and Doyle sticks his torso out. I get ready to run, in case he comes after me.

'Where the fuck are you going now?'

'Away from you and your racist gobshite.'

He slams the door.

I need to be on my own to think things through properly, calmly, without Doyle fucking with my head, so I head into the old plantation. Deep in the trees, so deep it's difficult to find, even when you know it's there, is the ruin of a croft. The plantation must have grown up around it as its roof gave in to gravity and time. By the time I have fought my way through the undergrowth, the sun is out. I stand in the humid air of the clearing for a moment, close my eyes and turn my face towards the sun. Around me are the sounds of birdsong and water dripping heavily from the trees.

The walls of the old house are broken by three small

windows and a narrow doorway. A hearth at one end of the single room is the only other feature. The grass-covered floor is littered with stones from the collapsing masonry. I turn one over to use its dry side as a seat and retrieve my tin from the chimney. Inside is a small, nearly empty bottle of whisky, two porn mags and a couple of ready-made joints.

Soon, they'll search the woods. Men in fluorescent jackets walking through the trees in slow-moving lines. When they do, they'll find this place. They'll use it against me, insinuate things.

I light a joint and have a last, affectionate look through the magazines before pulling out the pages one at a time and making a fire of them. Staring, stoned, into the flames, I watch disembodied limbs and genitals blacken and disappear.

I poke at the ash with a stick while I finish the whisky. Looking around me, it's easy to believe the forest has been here forever, but Doyle reckons it was planted in the thirties. The people who lived in this little stone house could never have guessed that one day it would be lost beneath the trees. There could be a hundred houses like this one hidden under the trees for all I know. For all anyone knows. Even so, when I first found the croft, there was a rusty beer can, so I knew somebody else was here once, unless the ghosts that live here have a taste for cheap lager. Not that I believe in ghosts. There is no such thing as a soul. Nothing after we die. The girl in the loch could tell you that.

It is dark by the time I get back and my jeans are covered in mud from trying to find my way down the lane without a torch. I am afraid to go back into the caravan, but I'm not about to sleep in the barn just because of Doyle.

I try to go in quietly, but the ill-fitting door and rusty metal step both squeal. They might as well be a burglar alarm, but inside the 'van is silent. Doyle's bedroom door is shut. I creep up to it, putting my ear slowly to the thin panel of the door.

'Doyle?' I whisper. 'You awake?'

'I am now.'

'Are you okay?'

'Get t' bed, for fuck's sake.'

I can't sleep. I'm still wound up and my midge bites are itching something fierce, so I lie in my bed listening to heavy drops falling from the trees above and hitting the metal roof like ball bearings. The kitchen tap, dripping softly into the steel sink, echoes the tapping on the roof.

I'm still awake when Doyle gets up for a slash. He's thick-set and heavy, but he treads lightly. Even so, the van's old floor panels groan under his weight and the door squeals against its frame. I listen to his piss hitting the grass outside. A moment later there is a brief flare in the darkness as he lights a fag. The night air carries a chilling wave of dampness through the caravan, bringing first the smell of wet pine and bracken and then the smell of Doyle's fag.

'Doyle?'

'What?'

'I'm sorry about what I called you. I didn't mean it.'

'It doesn't matter. I get mouthy after a drink. Get to sleep.'

I pull the thin sleeping bag tighter around me. I feel better for a while, but when I close my eyes, I dream of the girl. The bloating from the water has made her look fatter than she had been in life, so she is almost unrecognisable. Her skin is greasy looking, and taut, as though it might split. The water is dark and she is so white she seems almost to glow in the gloom beneath the trees. Not like when I'd see her working at the chippy; always hot and pink, sweat glistening in her cleavage.

When I wake, Doyle is standing in his Y-fronts, pouring beans from a catering-size tin into a pan. 'Beans,' he says, and drops a bowl on the table as I slump into the seat. Instead of sitting down opposite me, he perches his old carcass on the counter, his crotch level with my face while I am trying to eat. As he gobbles his food out of the pan, I can see his cock bobbing under the ancient fabric of his pants.

'Not hungry?'

'No. I'll have mine later. Ta though.'

'Watching your weight, eh?'

He lets out a long, disinterested fart before going back into the bedroom to get dressed.

Before Doyle comes out of his room, I hear the sound of Pavel's clattering truck in the lane. He doesn't come out this way often. He must be here to see us, the lane doesn't go anywhere else, but I still jump when he bangs on the door. By the time I open it he is already staring impatiently through the kitchen window. I lean around the door frame and he turns to face me, picking mud from his overalls as he speaks.

'Why don't you answer your phones. It's a pain in my arse driving up here.'

'No signal,' I lie.

'I've got signal. Why haven't you?'

Doyle appears at my shoulder smelling of booze and cheap soap. 'Pavel, my friend. What can we do for you, sir?'

'The road around the loch is off limits.'

'Oh, and why might that be?'

'Police. Doing something.'

'What?'

'The work crew found something.'

My mouth is going dry. 'I wonder if it's those townies been up to something.'

Pavel looks at me like I'm an idiot. 'Townies? Why would they be there?'

'I bet it's them.'

'Bet what's them?'

'Whatever it is . . .'

'Whatever . . . I just came to tell you, stay out of the way. They will be up to see you, soon I think.'

'Us? Why us?'

'They question all the workers. Okay. See you. Goodbye.'

As Pavel starts his engine, Doyle waves him off and closes the door. 'Wanker.' He takes a beer from the fridge and starts guzzling it. 'Well now, that's interesting, isn't it?'

'I suppose so.' I shrug, trying to look as though I don't care. He sits opposite me at the little table. I have the sudden sense he knows what is in the water, that he's known all along, that he's been playing with me.

'You been up at the loch recently?' He leans forward, too interested in my reply for me to be comfortable. I feel my face reddening.

'No. Why'd you say that?'

'No reason.'

'Why ask then?'

'Just curious.'

'Have you?'

'What?'

'Been up there?'

'What's it to you?'

He has been there, I can tell. He's making too much eye contact. The shifty bastard never looks you in the eye unless he's up to something or trying to psych you out.

'Thought you might know what it's all about.'

'No. Why would I?'

'I just thought . . .'

Doyle has a slight smile on his face. 'Sure there isn't something you want to tell me?'

Outside, I hear the sound of a car approaching slowly down the lane, crunching over the gravel and splashing through the puddles. I can tell by the engine it isn't Pavel's clapped-out truck. Doyle can't help himself, his eyes flicker towards the window. I see him swallow hard. They're not going to care what happened. They will just need someone to pin it on. They're coming.

I'm sweating now.

I need to get a grip. I take a long slow breath, flatten my voice and look him right in the eye. 'Doyle..?'

'What?'

'You never told me what you were inside for.'

He pauses mid gulp, a breathy burp hissing into the half-empty tin. There is a long silence while we stare at each other across a mile of sticky Formica. The morning sun bleeds through the mildewed, orange fabric of the curtain bathing everything in a deep, warm light and catching Doyle's eyes as he squints at me. I guess he's trying to remember what he's got on me and wondering what I've got on him. Slowly he puts his beer down. 'Tell me again about all these townies that have been coming up here making trouble . . .'

Empty Rooms

4 Fieldhead Avenue, Brizemore Village, Nr. Darnforth

T HE FRONT DOOR opens into the hallway and cool, autumn air surges across the threshold. The first steps Danny and Andrea take into a new house are always reverential, quieted by the sense that they are entering a space that is not theirs.

'Who lived here?' he asks.

'An old woman. Ex-headmistress.'

'Not from our school?'

'Don't think so.'

'Why'd she move?'

'Died.'

'Here . . .?'

Andrea looks at him sideways, pulls a face. 'Maybe it's haunted,' she says, and they laugh.

Every week or so, she flicks through her mother's folders and appointment diary. There are always one or two properties on the company's books that are unoccupied. Behind the emptiness is always unhappiness – a death or a repossession. There are a lot of repossessions – these are hard times and Darnforth is not a rich town. Once Andrea has selected a house, she takes the keys from an envelope in the filing cabinet and picks up her phone.

Beyond the enclosing walls of their secret playgrounds, they hardly meet, but every day Danny waits for the soft ping of an incoming text to prick the deadening bubble around him. He always goes. He doesn't care if it means skipping school or ditching his Saturday job at the warehouse. It doesn't matter to him if his A-levels falter, or if he's sacked.

'Oh my god, I'm soaked,' she says, peeling off her jacket and dropping her bag to the floor. Her voice echoes against the bare walls as she wanders into the kitchen, and he watches her tracing the wall with her fingertips as she goes.

'Handmade, Italian tiles. Nice.'

'How do you know?'

'You get an eye for these things if your parents are estate agents.'

There is no furniture left. The empty spaces of the house stretch unbroken beneath high ceilings with ornate coving.

'Original features,' she says. 'Good selling point.'

Only the shapes pressed into the faded pile of the carpet betray the human history of the rooms: the ghosts of sofas and coffee tables. Limp, yellow leaves from the willow tree in the garden stick to the patio doors. There is a swimming pool outside, and a large garden hidden from the surrounding houses by a wall of conifers. The house was grand once, but now the tiles are falling off the wall, the water in the pool is green and when they try to go out to the patio, the sliding doors stick in their runners. The weak morning sunshine seems to be the afterglow of the summer's brighter days. Both the house, and the light that fills it, belong to another time.

In the room referred to in the estate agent's particulars as 'Reception Room 2', is an abandoned, upright piano – too big to move, perhaps. Danny can't resist playing a few notes, each one rupturing the silence, hanging in the air, merging with the next. As the vibration of the last note sinks back into the quiet, the phone rings. They both jump, Andrea letting out a small scream, and they begin sniggering.

'Answer it,' he says, grinning at her.

'No way.'

'Go on!'

'No.'

But she is already looking at the receiver of the still-ringing phone and he knows she's thinking about it. In a quick movement that takes her off guard, he lifts the receiver and throws it to her and, caught by surprise and still stifling giggles, she gingerly answers, 'Hello?' There is a long pause. 'Who is this?' She seems suddenly serious, the flush of laughter draining from her cheeks. The room is silent again as she quietly puts the receiver back in its cradle.

'Who was it?'

'I don't know. Some guy.'

'What did he want?'

'I don't know. Nothing really. It was a bad line and he seemed surprised when I answered, like he thought there wouldn't be anyone here.'

'So why call?'

'How should I know. He seemed confused. Maybe he was a nutter?'

'We'd better go.'

'No, it'll be okay. We can just keep a look out.'

'If it's okay, why are you looking so freaked out?'

'He knew my name.'

'Fuck. He knew you? Who was it?'

'I told you, I don't know!'

'Someone from school?'

'No, he was way older than that.'

'How much older?'

'Really old. Sounded at least thirty or forty or something. I couldn't tell properly. I didn't recognise him. Maybe someone my mum works with.'

They are unnerved for a while, watching the door, listening for the crunch of feet on the shingle outside, but no one comes, and the fear is always part of the fun. Andrea is careful to choose houses that nobody will be viewing, but there is always a chance they will be discovered. They are always ready to run, and an exit route is always planned. Only once, when they were bunking off school, had they experienced the dreaded sound of key-in-lock, the held breath, and the panicked, giggling dash for the back gate, as an agent showed his clients into the hallway.

They both like the risk, but Andrea likes the houses too. She's finds something in them he can't. He sees it in the way she moves through the rooms, letting her hands linger in the places that other people have touched. She fingers light switches, cupboard handles and curtain pulls. She leans against walls, fitting her shoulder against grazed wallpaper where others have brushed past a thousand times, and she flicks through piled junk mail, tracing the names printed on the envelopes, imagining other lives.

They explore, they drink some beers, and they dance to the stereo they have brought with them. The smell of rain-damp air still clings to them. The stereo's tinny voice fills the room, but barely travels beyond its threshold. The syrupy music and this sudden, longed-for proximity feed the ache that has been building in each of them since the last house. Danny unfastens their roll-mats and throws them on the floor.

'No! Not there.' Andrea laughs and runs upstairs. 'Come on!'

He picks up their stuff and follows, but more slowly. There is always a strange moment when they go upstairs, into the bedrooms, as though the one-time residents might still be in there, quietly sleeping the afternoon away.

They strip and hang their clothes on the doors to dry and run back to their hastily-made bed, pulling his sleeping bag across their goose-bumped skin.

17 Albert Road, Darnforth

Although each new house feels different, their routine is the same: explore, drink beer – or cheap wine – and listen to music. They play the 'if this was our place . . .' game, arranging imaginary furniture and imagining a future life where everything is as it should be, and they fit an imaginary social life around successful, fantasy careers.

They make love then doze for a while, unworried about

being missed – his parents are pleasantly, stupidly, trusting, and hers are never home long enough to notice – but they are careful not to fall asleep, not properly, no matter how late they stay. The threat of an unexpected visit from an agent or a maintenance man keeps the young lovers alert so, as the time slips past, they lie awake, ready to be re-energised by a touch.

In the bedroom they have chosen – she has chosen – there is an impression in the carpet where a bed has been. They could sleep anywhere but she puts their roll-mat and sleeping bags within the outline. Tonight, there is no dancing and little conversation, time is short. They are leaving earlier now. The evenings are encroaching into the grey sunlight of the chill October afternoons. The houses, always cold in their forlorn wait for new owners, are growing colder. They daren't risk using the heating, or even the lights, for fear of discovery.

In the gloom at the end of the roll-mats, two chairs are turned towards them as though seated spectators are observing their movements. Danny wonders why she can't see this; why the space watching them doesn't disturb her. He finds himself looking for movement in the shadows, trying to catch the watchers from the corner of his eye. Finally, their invisible presence is too much. He stretches across their makeshift nest to push the chairs away, breaking their line of sight.

4 Fieldhead Avenue, Brizemore Village, Nr. Darnforth

This is the only place they have come back to more than

once. It's been a few weeks since their first visit, but Danny doesn't like it. The strange phone call the last time they were here still troubles him. He considers pulling the phone out of the wall so there won't be any more calls but, when he picks up the phone, the line is dead, disconnected. Before he can replace the receiver, Andrea takes it from him, and he watches her touch redial and listen to nothing on the dead line.

It isn't just the phone call that unsettles him though. There is something about the building itself that he finds disquieting. Maybe the potential buyers feel it too because there has been no interest in the house all summer. Andrea loves it.

'I'm so gonna live here one day, or somewhere like it.'

'It's creepy.'

'It's beautiful. It just needs some TLC.'

Later, when they're lying on their roll-out bed and they're sort of fucking, sort of talking, he is on edge. He worries that the man on the phone knew Andrea, knew somehow that she would be in the house, and as he tries and fails to make sense of it, twinges of fear and jealousy trouble him. Andrea too seems distant, only half aware of what she is doing. The house has cast a spell across them, filling their ears and eyes with dust and weighting down their tongues with thoughts and suspicions that can't quite be gathered together. She reaches across to a low shelf where an old pictureless frame lies broken, and caresses it with her fingertips as though it were a cherished heirloom.

'In Japan they have a shrine for the God of Broken Things,' she tells him.

'Why?'

'Because they believe everything has a spirit, and if they're forgotten, their god gets angry.'

45b Market Street, Darnforth

Danny stands in the window looking down into the road, a tributary of the high street, watching the occasional passers-by. Behind him, Andrea is asleep on their bed. They have been at this too long and they are becoming complacent. The notion of being caught seems more remote these days. Sometimes they risk sleep and wake disorientated by the faded smells of other people's lives: food, tobacco, sometimes a hint of laundry detergent or floor cleaner. Once there had been perfume, heady and old-fashioned, an oily tidemark on the carpet showing where it had been spilled, leaving a scent-ghost of its wearer lingering in the air.

This flat has been empty for months. There is a stick-iness to the surfaces, and a faint but unpleasantly human smell, as though the previous occupants have been dissolved and sprayed in a fine layer onto everything around them. The autumn wind gusting down the chimney fills the room with the smell of things that were burnt a long time ago.

Quietly, Danny lies down beside Andrea. He should wake her – it's time to leave – but he keeps quiet and takes her hand. She stirs but doesn't open her eyes. A week ago, not far from this flat, outside a bar on the high street, he'd watched from a distance as she talked to an older guy who was leaning out of a car window. Danny was with friends;

they were being turned away from a nightclub by bouncers
– *Got any ID's lads? No? Fuck off then.* Danny didn't care.
He had lost interest in the club. He watched her across the
market square, standing beside the car, hip pushed out,
head tipped to one side, smiling, trying too hard to impress
this man who he'd never seen.

4 *The Street, Brizemore Village, Nr. Darnforth*

Three hours ago, she gave him the keys and said, 'Wait for
me there. I'll come as soon as I can.'

Danny is nervous. He distrusts the house anyway, and
a third visit feels like they're pushing their luck. This is
the first time he's arrived without Andrea, and, without
her, his courage is flagging. The last time they were here,
the trees and tall hedges surrounding the house brought
a feeling of sanctuary, but now that he's alone, they only
seem to isolate the house from its surroundings.

None of that matters though, there is no chance that
he'll leave. If he does, he will lose her. He knows they can't
go on stealing time in the unreal world they've built, but it's
all they have. Their visits have already become only occasional. Andrea says there are fewer houses on the market in
winter, but he senses she's losing interest, or maybe playing
their game with someone else. Despite himself, he thinks
of the caller again.

It is twilight, the end of November, but he dares not
turn on a light. Sitting on the stairs of the darkening house
he listens to a wind-blown thicket of bamboo outside the
window as it taps and scratches at the glass. Without

Andrea he feels like a burglar, even though there is only
dust to steal. He's not even a good burglar; alone, he doesn't
even have the courage to move deeper into the building, so
he lingers in the hallway. Around him he feels the empty
rooms of the house and the traces of all the lives that have
moved through them. He feels suddenly uncomfortable
sitting with his back to the dusky space at the top of the
stairs, as though he's being watched, and he shifts position
to lean against the wall.

In the semi-darkness, time melts away. The colours of
the house mute to Payne's grey, and the gloom gathering
in the rooms beyond the hall seems heavy, almost liquid.
The shadow into which the house is sinking is cold and
Danny feels as though something is about to happen, as
though an unseen fuse has been lit somewhere. He realises
he is trembling, or shivering, or both.

The stillness around him is shocked by a sharp and
sudden banging on the front door. He knows immediately it's not her. She would knock quietly, stealthily. This
thumping – the side of a fist against the heavy wood
– booms down the hallway. A shadow appears in the
distorted glass of the door, tall and broad. Danny freezes,
holding his breath, praying the visitor won't look through
the letterbox which opens directly in front of the stairs
where he is sitting. He slides slowly around the corner, into
the lounge. There is movement outside the window and
the tread of feet on the gravel path. He flattens himself
quickly against the wall, still hardly breathing, and turns
his head, straining to see. Behind the gauze of the old net
curtains a man is peering into the room, face pressed to
the glass, looking for something, or someone. He stares

directly at Danny but seems not to see him, perhaps seeing only his own reflection, or the darkness of the room's interior.

There is something familiar about the man but, try as he might, Danny can't place him. Unwilling to chance being spotted, he doesn't risk a proper look. Perhaps the stranger is looking for Andrea. Maybe she knows him, he thinks coldly. Maybe this is her mystery caller. He wonders for a moment if it's the same guy he saw Andrea flirting with in town, but the silhouette on the other side of the glass is bigger, his hair darker.

Outside, the man is shouting something, but his voice seems muffled, as though underwater, and all Danny can think of is getting away. He tiptoes upstairs and into a box room above the hall. Standing to one side of the window, he peers around the edge of the lopsided blind. Below him, the man is looking up. Danny pulls back quickly into the room, heart pounding, and stays out of sight until he feels bold enough to push the blind aside for another look – more cautious this time – and finds the man is gone.

Danny moves warily through the house, checking the windows and doors on the ground floor. He has started to relax a little when another knock on the front door sets his heart racing again. He tucks himself into a corner, away from the windows, as he hears the letter box rattle, then Andrea calling out to him.

Standing in the open doorway, she realises something is wrong before he says anything.

'What happened?'

'Someone was here.'

'Who?'

'I don't know. Some guy.'

'Did he see you?'

'No. I don't know. Maybe.'

As Andrea steps across the threshold, Danny suddenly feels certain that if they stay in this house something bad will happen. He doesn't know where the feeling is coming from, or if it has anything to do with the man, and he knows if he tries to explain it she'd laugh at him. 'We should go. He might come back.'

'What did he want?'

'I don't know. I wasn't going to talk to him, was I?' he says, but he can't shake the feeling that he'd been looking for Andrea.

As they leave, she makes him describe the visitor. He tells her in as much detail as he is able, watching carefully for any signs of recognition. She doesn't react, or even look at him while he talks. She seems angry, as though the whole thing is his fault, as though he has spoiled something.

'You weren't expecting someone, were you?' he asks, carefully.

'Of course not.'

'I thought it might be someone you knew.'

'Don't be stupid.'

'Like the phone call, remember?'

'What about the phone call?'

'He knew you, didn't he, the guy. Knew you'd be here.'

'Well, I didn't know him.'

'OK.'

'OK? What's that supposed to mean?'

'I don't know. I think maybe it means you might have come here with someone else.'

'Oh, fuck off.'

They walk back to town together but after that afternoon, she stops calling him. There are no more texts. No more addresses. She dodges out of sight and disappears from his life. He knows she's still around – he hears things when, from time to time, someone he knows bumps into her, and he catches fragmentary news from mentions on social media, but he never sees Andrea again. Sometimes, over the years, he thinks he glimpses her in the street or a bar, but he doesn't quite trust his memory and maybe it's just someone who looks like her. Sometimes, even years later, he dreams about her.

He hears of her death from an old school friend, and he goes back to visit the houses they went to together. It takes him a long time to find some of them because, in his absence, the town has changed a lot. The houses are different now, all occupied, and through the windows he can see rooms cluttered with furniture. There are kids shouting in the gardens, and cars in the driveways, in all but one.

4 Fieldhead Avenue, Brizemore Village, Nr. Darnforth

Daniel phones the estate agent to arrange a viewing. He arrives early and makes his way up the drive. Even after so long, the house seems familiar. The gardens have been re-landscaped, but the beds are overgrown and the lawns uncut. The estate agent is late and Danny wonders if she might be waiting inside. The doorbell doesn't work so he bangs on the heavy front door with the side of his fist. There is no response, but he thinks he hears movement inside and moves to look through the living-room window. He can see no one, but he senses that there is someone there, he feels watched. He steps back into the driveway and his eye is drawn by a movement at the window of the room above the front door. He is about to go around to the back of the house to see if he can find a way in when the estate agent arrives. Apologising for being late, she fishes for the house keys in her bag.

He barely recognises the house inside. It's brighter, the high hedges around it have been cut back to let light in. Sunlight pours in through curtain-less windows. The rooms are smaller than he remembers them, but they are as empty now as they were when he first came here with Andrea. Beneath the kitchen counters are voids where white goods had stood, plumbing connections left hanging like severed limbs. The handmade Italian tiles are still there. He smiles, remembering them, pleased that she kept them.

He lets the estate agent lead him through the house. In the master bedroom, Danny pictures Andrea with her husband, and he wonders if she ever told him about the times they had spent there. The estate agent looks out of the window and talks about the desirable aspect of the property and ample off-street parking. Daniel asks for a moment to think, and the agent tells him she'll be downstairs.

Alone, he wanders through the upstairs rooms. He imagines Andrea walking just behind him, asking, 'Do you think anyone died here?'

Looking around him, he replies to her, out loud, 'No.' His voice only barely breaks the silence. 'No way.'

'Maybe it's haunted,' she says.

In the bathroom a dusty brown trail meanders down the bath where a moth has landed in water pooled below a dripping tap and flopped its way along the enamel. In the children's room, with its bruised and crayon-marked wallpaper, the scruffy carpet and beaten skirting boards hint at the happy chaos of family life and mark the passing of time more clearly than days ticked off a calendar.

From the top of the stairs, he looks down into the hall-way, flooded with crisp sunlight, painted in off-whites and pale greys. It's difficult to imagine it as it was, but he can still see himself sitting at the bottom of the stairs, afraid to turn around, and of what might be up here in the shadows.

He finds himself looking for something – a sign that she had ever been there – half expecting to find a memento of the time they had spent together, but there is nothing. The part of his life he'd shared with her was no more than a blink, an image that flickered across the walls of empty houses during a single, long summer thirty years ago. He barely knew her at all, but he can see her everywhere, as she was then. Her voice seems to hang in the sunlight, like a piano note echoing through the empty house.

Danny goes back to the lounge where the estate agent is waiting for him, and they talk for a while about the house and its history. 'It's so sad,' she tells him, 'to see a home that had been loved so much standing empty like this.'

As they leave, Danny glances back into the room and the telephone on the windowsill catches his eye. On a whim he crosses the floor and, smiling, lifts the receiver from its cradle. The line is silent, holding its breath, waiting for voices from other places to return.

'Disconnected,' the agent tells him.

He is about to return the handset to its cradle when he hears something. He holds his breath, listens . . .

Static? A breeze passing over an open microphone? Breathing?

Amongst the static, broken and indistinct, there is a voice . . .

'Hello . . .?'

The Memory System

I AM TOLD that I spent only two months in the half-light world of my grandfather. I was eight and it was the first time I'd seen a city at night. Curled on the back seat amongst blankets, looking up at the coloured lights of show rooms, office blocks and shops as they passed above me, the drive to the other side of town was the longest trip I'd been on. But it wasn't only the neons and shop signs that made an impression on me: until that night, I'd never met my grandfather. The first time I knew of his existence was when my mother started to get ill. When she phoned him, I knew she was nervous. I listened as she tried to whisper into the mouthpiece, but crying at the same time meant her words were almost shouted through clenched teeth: 'You've got to take her. Just for a while.'

When we got to his place, on the top floor of a small block, he must have forgotten we were coming; my mother had to bang on the door for a long time before it opened, just a crack, and his face appeared behind the chain, masked by a hat and scarf as though he was about to go out in a blizzard. Back then, as I was handed across the threshold, I was old enough to see things, but not old enough to understand. He looked at her the way you'd look at a stranger, not the way you'd look at your own child.

Inside, the flat was sealed in permanent twilight; every window had been covered with a patchwork of black cloth fixed in position with glue and tape, and the lights stayed on all day and all night. The hallway and the room beyond it, that would have served as a living room in a more conventional flat, were lit by a dozen chains of Christmas lights strung around the walls and along the tops of furniture. They filled the flat with a warm glow and left its corners in deep shadow. Only the kitchen had conventional lighting; a single fluorescent tube cast its grey light over the worn plastic veneers of chipboard furniture.

My memory of those first few days of night is vague. I don't remember how long I cried, but my fear of the dark flat and the stranger with whom I'd been abandoned impossibly far away from home made me inconsolable. For a long time I sat crying by the front door where I'd watched my mother walk away and, when I'd exhausted myself, my grandfather made a bed for me on the sofa, piling up old sleeping bags that smelled of a dog he had once owned. Unable to tell whether it was day or night, I couldn't tell how long I slept, but later, lying awake, sobbing again, I heard him crying on the other side of a closed door. When you're a kid it seems worse when adults cry, more significant somehow, and in my curiosity, I stopped crying so I could listen to him. We spent the first night on opposite sides of a plasterboard wall, each curled in our loneliness and each scared of the other. I missed the turbulent presence of my mother, despite everything she'd done, and everything she'd failed to do.

On the first day, he told me the rules. I sat on my sofa-bed while he looked me in the eyes and told me the two things I must never do.

'Number one: never open the front door to anyone. And, number two,' pointing towards what I'd presumed was his bedroom, 'never open that door. Never look in, or go inside. Unless I take you in. Understand?'

At first, I stayed as close to my bed as I could, seeking some kind of security by piling the covers around me. My corner of the room was brightened by the light from an old black and white television that my grandfather dragged out and placed on top of a wooden crate for me. While I watched television he'd disappear for hours at a time into the closed room.

I settled into a new routine, fitting myself without protest around the movements of my grandfather as he lumbered around the dark rooms. My fear of him ebbed away, dissolving into the soft shadows. I knew he was strange, but I'd been used to living with my mother's state of constant desperation and I'd learned to accept things as they were. It was a long time before I found out how a mother was supposed to behave or what a normal life felt like.

I began to explore my new world. In time I found that some of the material used to black out the windows was loose. I picked at the covering and tape with tiny fingers, finding gaps that bigger, clumsier hands wouldn't have found, until I made a hole. I'd become accustomed to the dark and I was surprised when a beam of daylight burst through. Holding my eye to the light I was able to see over the roof tops of the houses that stood in front of the flats and down the main road beyond. After that I'd wait for grandfather to go into the kitchen or his room and peel back tiny sections of tape and fabric to peep through the gaps at the bright world outside.

As I grew more comfortable with the old man, I began to ask him if my mother was okay and when she'd be coming back for me. It was typical of her that she'd sent no word to either of us. He'd answer: 'She's fine,' and, 'Soon'.

I'd been brought up to look after myself, so that's what I did. He told me I didn't have to go to school anymore and I spent the days playing amongst the junk and old furniture piled around the rooms of the flat, wearing costumes made from the old clothes I found jammed into sacks. Once I'd grown used to the warm glow of the Christmas lights, the flat seemed less haunted. I had to be quiet as I played though. It wasn't one of the rules, but Grandfather said any noise would annoy the family of rats downstairs. He told me the whole block was full of rats, and the ones downstairs, along with another family down the landing, were the worst. It took a while for me to figure out that when he spoke about 'Rats' he meant the other tenants in the block.

Later he showed me the spy hole in the front door where I could watch them. Standing on a chair dragged from the kitchen, with my eye pressed to the tiny bubble of glass, I was fascinated how distant people seemed when they stood in the narrow landing beyond the door. If I was playing and heard anyone in the passageway, I'd run for my chair and, as silently as possible, climb up to see the postman pushing letters through the door or watch the Rats standing, as they often did, at the top of the stairwell, shouting to each other and spitting down the shaft between the flights of stairs. My grandfather was happy to play along, whispering, 'Keeping an eye on the Rats?' or 'Guard duty? Good girl.' I'd nod gravely, happy to do something important, and make a show of checking all the locks and chains he'd fitted to the inside of the door.

There was rarely any proper food in the flat; we only ever seemed to eat tins of spaghetti hoops and drink cherryade. I was never able to tell if that was what he liked to eat or if he'd bought them because he thought that was what kids ate. I asked him once why there was no toast or cornflakes like we had at home. He told me he didn't keep that kind of thing in the flat because rats would come through the air ducts to eat them. On that occasion he meant real rats, but that night, and for days afterwards, I had nightmares about the brutal neighbours squeezing out of the narrow ventilation grill and forcing my grandfather to make them breakfast. In my nightmare, when they had eaten, they immediately vomited into the kitchen sink – by then I'd become used to seeing my mother vomit after meals.

Maybe we only had spaghetti hoops and cherryade once or twice. Memory does strange things over the years. Maybe I just dreamt it, like the vomiting rat family. In any case, that is how I remember breakfast. Grandfather would insist we went out every night for exercise and fresh air, and to 'eat out'. He didn't like to go out during the day: 'Too many people', he said, and added, 'Better if people don't know you're staying here.'

When he did go out, he wore three coats and a wide-brimmed hat and scarf so only part of his face showed.

We'd leave the flats late at night and walk down the road I'd seen from my peephole at the window. It was about a mile to the bright light of an all-night food store, where I would wait outside, hiding myself in the alley next to the shop. When the old man came out with a bag of food, we'd walk on a little further, to a bench that overlooked a road junction where traffic lights ticked through their colour sequence all night in spite of the emptiness of the roads.

It felt nice to be out of the stale air of the sealed flat, but I hated sitting on the bench to eat our food. I hated it partly because I knew that normal people only had picnics in the daytime and partly because it was cold. When my mother left me, I had only a bag of summer clothes, so when it was really cold, Grandfather would take off one of the overcoats he wore and wrap it around me. His coats always smelled bad. I think even on those cold nights he must have been sweating a lot under the many layers he wore, but after a while I didn't notice it so much. If there was nobody else about, or if it rained, we would sit in the bus shelter. It was brightly lit by an advertising panel, and it kept out the worst of the cold when the wind sliced down the long stretch of glistening tarmac. When he thought I was sad, which was often, Grandfather would buy a box of chocolates and shake them at me. I could tell by his eyes that behind his scarf he was smiling.

If I complained about having to walk all the way back to the flat, he'd stand me on the bench next to him and point down the street to where the block of flats stood like a turret above the other houses. 'It's only there. We will be home in no time. It's no distance at all.' I'd keep looking up all the way back, waiting until I could see the black squares that were unmistakably the blanked-out windows of his flat.

That was twenty-five years ago, but I remember it with perfect clarity. Every night we followed the same route from the shop back to his flat, where we would lock the door five times to keep the Rats out. And now, in my mind's eye, I do the same walk every day.

I was first taught *the loci system* by a tutor while I studied for my degree. It is a way to recall things by placing them at specific locations in a mental recreation of a building, or along the path of a journey that you know well. To begin with, it is only useful for remembering short lists of items – shopping lists, that kind of thing – but over time you can expand it, use it to recall more complicated stuff. It works, with practice. I've had to work harder than most to get where I am, and it has helped that I never forget.

For the system to work properly, you have to be there in your mind. You have to imagine it so clearly you can feel it. After a while, using it every day, it becomes so much a part of you that you know it more intimately than you will ever know any other journey. When the tutor told me that it would be easier to recall the images if I attached them to an environment I'd known since childhood, I was immediately back on the dark road, holding onto my grandfather, following the same walk that we'd done every night, and every night I was scared. The journey I make in my mind now is a distillation of all those nights that I lived in grandfather's world.

To recall things, you must begin in the same place and follow the same route each time. Mine starts, as it always did, at the bench where we would sit for our nightly feast of whatever junk food was left on the shelves at the end of the day's trading, eaten from greasy plastic wrappers. It's dark and always cold.

I make the things I need to remember part of the scene. Everything there appears as it was when I was eight; the way I will always see it. If, for example, I had to remember to pick up a pair of shoes from the menders, a pair of shoes would be there on the bench, but they wouldn't be the shoes of a woman in her thirties; the shoes I would see there have been kicked off by a child, one on the bench and one on the floor, laces trailing into a puddle.

The second location is the public telephone that stood along the road. For a long time I used this point to remind me to call my mother, so much so that she became part of the image, and even now, years after her death, she's still hanging around the phone box. As I approach, she is crying, because in this landscape from my childhood, that is how she always appears. It used to frighten me, but now I pity her. Once she'd become a permanent addition to the scene, her wailing began to annoy me, so I turned the sound off and now she carries on in silence. The phone box itself is brightly lit, but so dirty you can barely see through the windows. Anything I have to remember here is on the shelf next to the phone, or my mother holds it out towards me.

Then, I move on to the next location: the fire escape next to the food store, where I waited for my grandfather to finish shopping. When my feet were hurting after the long walk from the flat, I would go through a gate into the alley-way where stairs led up to the second floor of the building.

I would sit on the step, afraid to look down the alleyway behind me, until my grandfather's darkly-wrapped bulk filled the gateway and beckoned to me. When I use this location to remember something, it is always placed on the third step, just where a small child with tired feet would sit. I always look at it and turn quickly back out of the gate because under the stairs, even after all these years, there is still something moving in the dark.

Fifty yards further down the road stands an empty pub. I see it as it was when I was a little girl, partly derelict, its windows boarded with metal sheets. I never went inside as a child, but in the memory system, the door is ajar. Inside are the monsters that my mother assured me waited for naughty children inside all derelict buildings. They keep to the shadows, and as long as I stay in the light from the doorway, I know I'll be okay. If I need to remember an object, I see it placed on the bar; if I need to recall a person, I seat them on a barstool at the end of the bar, like a punter in the pub from hell. The person or the object is always illuminated in a small, harsh pool of light, like the one made by a cheap video camera.

Over the years I have added many more places along the road, each one burned into my memory on the night walks that terrified me as a kid, and reinforced now with daily use. The fear I felt as a child helps me to picture those places, bringing them into sharper focus than the other vague memories of my childhood. Like the steps in front of one of the grander houses, where, as we passed one night, a figure appeared behind the textured glass of the door. It's there now, whenever I go back, looking out, face pressed to the glass, and although its features are broken into globular distortions, I know it's watching over whatever object I've placed there, just as I saw it watching my grandfather and me as we passed all those years ago.

At its top end, the road bends to the left and on the other side a footpath carries on straight ahead, leading between rows of small, boxy houses to the flats beyond. Before we cross the road, there is a tall, red post box, its mouth sloping downwards at exactly the right angle for a small girl to stare into the dark interior. Anything I remember here is wedged into the slot or leaning against the exterior of the pillar box with a stamp on it. This is also the point in my journey where I pause to gather my courage before we approach the flats, just as I used to then.

Where the path goes along the back of the tiny houses, past fences and rows of bins, a gang of kids wait for us. Every time I revisit them, they are the same: unlearning, vile. The thugs make a surprisingly good place to remember something; the image of them is always vivid in my mind. One of them makes a lunge for the brim of Grandfather's hat, but he ducks out of the way before the kid can grab it. The boy just laughs and shouts, 'Yeehaw! There's a new sheriff in town, boys!' One of the others throws a beer can at him as we walk past, and I feel him pull me closer to him, protecting me, but I can tell he's scared and he doesn't make a sound until their laughter and shouts have faded and we're at the entrance to the flats.

The first time we passed the gang, all those years ago, I remember that I didn't know what to say, but I wanted him to feel better. All I could think of saying was, 'Don't worry, Granddad.' I repeat this mantra each time we encounter them, and I press his hand to my cheek, always surprised that it isn't rough as I expect from its appearance, but smooth and soft.

And then we're back at the stairs. One of the Rats sits on the second landing, ignoring us, running his hand across the stubble on his head and playing with a lighter as he hungrily covets whatever object I've placed at this location.

Passing the Rat Boy, I climb the stairs to the last landing, opposite my grandfather's front door. This is the next location: the pale green door to the flat where one of the Rats, maybe the one from the stairwell, has written 'purvurt' across the door with a marker pen. I ask him what it means and he tells me that it means 'people don't like it if someone is different to them.'

'Why don't you live somewhere else, if they don't like you?'

'I can't.'

I ask why, but he doesn't answer.

If I need to remember more, I go past the rubbish piled in the corridor and into the flat itself. Each time I come back, it is necessary to follow the route, and its sequence of locations, in the same order, just as it is outside, to make sure nothing is missed. The first place within the flat is the inside of the door: one peephole, two chains and three locks. One, two, three. The locks and chains arranged alternately down one side, glistening in the fake cosiness of the half-light, and Grandfather's warning hangs in the damp air: 'Never open the door to anyone.'

He takes off his hat and the two outermost coats, and the smell of unwashed body and damp wool surrounds me. Unwinding his scarf, he reveals his kind, round face; a face you would trust; one that I trusted. He drops the scarf onto a chair that always sits half buried by discarded clothes beside the door, marking the next point in my game. That, in turn, is followed by the table with the phone on it. Here I see Grandfather summoning the courage he needs to make a call, pacing around the hallway and rehearsing what he has to say. The call doesn't go according to rehearsal. He panics, hangs up and tells himself that it's better to try again later.

There's nothing else in the hallway, so the next locations I use are split between the bathroom and the kitchen. Both next to each other, both spotless, under-used and smelling of bleach. The next room is a bedroom, but it contains only one memory location because the little girl of my memory is afraid to go in there; the light doesn't work and junk is piled so deeply that it is only just possible to open the door. Anything I have to remember here stands inside the doorway on the only clear patch of carpet.

Then the hallway opens into the living room. My room. The room where my make-shift bed and television sit beneath the window with holes picked in its covering. The room where I wake sometimes to find him standing behind the sofa, watching me before he goes back into his room and closes the door firmly behind him. I wonder if he sleeps at all. When I sense it's time to get up, I play quietly behind my junk-built walls, dressed up in old clothes, until Grandfather emerges from his room growling and scratching himself. I'm still a little scared as he approaches and picks me up, but I find myself giggling until he says, 'Right, that's enough, put your old granddad down,' and he carefully places me back on my feet. He only really scares me when he stares at me with his clear blue eyes and reminds me of the rule, 'Never open that door without my say so,' and I know he will never say so.

The room, his room, is the last point in my system, but anything I have to remember here has to stay outside too. My memories from the other side of the door are too strong, too tied up with my grandfather to be used for this game. Or maybe it's because even now, part of me is afraid of disobeying his instructions and going inside. I think he would've liked that. But sometimes I allow myself to venture in again, in spite of the rule. I go in just to see, as I did all those years ago when my fear was finally beaten by my curiosity.

The door stands ajar and I can smell something: chemicals, something acidic. I push the door open a little further, just to see, and realise that the room isn't dark as I had first thought, but lit with a deep-red light. My eyes adjust and I can make out strange apparatus that later I will understand to be dark-room equipment. Grandfather is nowhere to be seen and I push the door open further and step inside, convinced he has gone somewhere else and my intrusion will go unnoticed. I stand in the dark, hardly daring to breath, surrounded by alien devices and the strange chemical-smelling air, and suddenly he's over me, from nowhere, emerging out of the darkness. I am terrified and begin to sob.

When he picks me up, I'm so afraid that I have to fight to gulp down air between sobs, until I realise that I'm not being punished or beaten, but hugged. He flicks a switch behind my head and suddenly the lights are on and the room is not terrifying and I can feel the vibrations of my grandfather's voice in his chest as he speaks to me. I recover my breath and wipe my eyes on my grandfather's shirt and I see that beyond the cameras and photographic enlargers we are surrounded on every wall by huge photographs. He lowers me to the ground, I walk up to the biggest of the pictures and all I can say is, 'Oh,' because I've not seen anything like it before. Each one is far taller than me. Almost all of them have been taken from the windows of the flat; I recognise the view from my peephole at the window in the room next door. In other pictures I recognise the surrounding streets. All at night. All dark. But not how it was when we walked down the road each evening: they are luminous, with pools of light flared by long exposures. Traces of people, where they'd lingered in front of the lights from shops, look like burning angels, and car headlights like comet trails. The sky is filled with a strange glow that emanates from the buildings below it, fading to a deep black above them. In the pictures I can see everything I knew from our nocturnal walks: the phone box, glowing in the dark; the traffic lights at the distant junction; the food store; the derelict pub, and everything else.

When my mother came to take me away again, he said to me, 'Promise to come back and see me. Now that your mum is better, it's no distance at all.' I told him I would, promised faithfully, but my mother never took me back. When he handed me to her at the door, he said quietly, 'Look after her.' She responded as she often did – as though she'd been accused of something – 'Course I'll look after her, she's my daughter.' A guilty conscience, probably. He had looked after me; even when he was so scared it made his voice shake, he always held me behind him, away from danger, and away from the Rats. I was less sure about my mother, but I was still glad when she came for me, excited even. I had longed to see her again. Longing not for the reality of the life she'd given me, but for what I hoped it might be.

When he died, my mother, cold and practical as ever, sold his cameras and other stuff. She was still comparatively young when she followed him to the grave and we never spoke about him or my time there. I never found out about his life or who – aside from being her father – he had been. She'd left him behind in some forgotten part of her life. It was just as well she died before I was able to leave her behind. I missed her a little when she had gone, but I don't think the rest of the world will, much. I used to worry that I'd drift into the same place that she'd followed her father into; a world of fear and dark places held together with frayed logic and drugs. It might be luck that I didn't take to my inheritance, but I know I'm stronger than my mother ever was.

If I'd never seen my grandfather's photographs and the other world he created in them, maybe I would've surrendered to my mother's lack of hope and I'd never have seen anything beyond the life she'd prepared for me. I don't know what happened to the pictures he made; I guess my mother sold them or threw them away with all the rest of his junk, but I still remember them as though they were in front of me. Once I had discovered them, I used to sit in front of them for hours, when Grandfather wasn't working, staring at the details and making up voices for the tiny glowing figures. I don't know if it's real or not, memory is a funny thing, but when I go back and follow the path from my past and I step through the last door to see the pictures he made, if I stare hard enough into the photograph, at the end of the street, in a flare of brilliant light that spills into the night from a store front, there is a bench where two tiny figures are sitting huddled together.

Sink

I DREAM ABOUT The Sink. From a drone's-eye perspective, I see it growing, yawning wider, drawing everything in; the world folding into itself, eroding to nothing, until the last fragments of creation disappear in a final trickle of sand.

I wake sweating, shaking, reaching for Jennifer. Then I remember she isn't there and I lie awake until the alarm goes off. I get up, shower, drink coffee, eat toast and leave for work. It is the same as any other day.

When I step outside it's already shockingly bright. Across the street Mrs Meyers is standing on her lawn in her dressing gown and a floral headscarf. She looks worried – more worried than usual, I mean.

'Hi, Mrs Meyers.'

'Have you seen Charlie?'

'Charlie?'

'My dog. My dog, Charlie.'

'No.'

She walks off towards the park.

I shout after her, 'If he's missing, I can help you find him . . .' But she doesn't look back.

I don't take offence. The people who stayed on after the evacuations tend to be a little eccentric. Also, if I'm being honest – which I'm trying to be – I resent Mrs Meyers and her dog. When Bilbo went missing, she didn't give a toss. I loved that mutt, although I admit I didn't want him at first. It was Jennifer who always wanted a dog. I knew she wouldn't look after it, so I said no. We got one anyway. When he disappeared, I hoped that it was because he missed Jen and he'd gone looking for her, like the dogs in kid's adventure films. I pictured him turning up on her doorstep, bedraggled but otherwise unharmed, but he never did. When Jen found out, she blamed me and that made things between us even worse. It's The Sink that's scaring the dogs away. They seem to sense it. Maybe they smell the scent of wet, dead earth, fathoms deep, carried on the breeze.

Not everyone left when they were supposed to, but apart from me and Mrs Meyers, there aren't many still living in our street. It's funny how some of us clung on, because there's nothing great about this part of the city. People got sentimental about it when they were told to ship out, old folks especially. They didn't want to leave places that had lifelong attachments – neighbourhoods where their families had grown up and they had grown old. A few people just didn't want to move, and some others couldn't afford to go, trapped by soaring rents further out of the city. They had to keep hoping that The Sink would stop growing before it reached the end of their garden. Like a lot of others, I took the government relocation money and then came back. Clever, right?

They were pretty hot on enforcing the evacuation at first, so we left the tape across the doors and stayed out of sight. But, as The Sink got bigger, so did their problems: protests, sit-ins, blah blah ... you know all this anyway. The police had better things to do than arrest some old dear who'd chained herself to the house she'd lived in for sixty years. So they gave up. We pulled the tape off the doors and carried on with our lives. Now we're all here, waiting it out, and it's kind of beautiful. Amongst the dereliction and boarded-up homes of the Perimeter Zone, you come across islands of order: the strangeness of a neatly-mowed lawn, a freshly-painted house, or a corner shop with its neon sign still flashing 'Open'. For some people, it's business as usual. They're still getting up, going to work, weeding the garden and hanging out their laundry.

◊

Everyone I know can recall when it first began, but not me. I barely remember it. It happened shortly after Jen left. It was a bad time for me. I was out of it for days, maybe weeks. What gets me now is the banality of it. The paying of bills, the who-owns-what, the leaving of her keys on the dining-room table and the sound of her car pulling out of the driveway as I kept my eyes on the TV, pretending not to care – *Star Trek*, in case you were wondering. The next day I had to go to work as though nothing had happened. I waved to Mrs Meyers as she took her dog for a walk and caught the bus like I did every Monday, and that was that. But somewhere downtown, not far from where I worked, near the tree-lined square where Jen and I would some-times meet for lunch, a road surface had started to sag and split.

By the time I caught up, what had started as a fleeting item at the end of the news broadcast had already blossomed into the headline story: a sinkhole that was large enough to swallow a whole intersection, then a nearby office block. All this in a city with no history of sinkholes, seismic activity, or any of that shit. For weeks you couldn't get close enough to see it; media trucks parked everywhere, roads closed, police standing around shouting into megaphones and putting up barriers. As the hole got deeper and wider, an endless stream of experts and cranks were interviewed in front of the new phenomenon. Only the crankiest of the cranks predicted it would keep growing.

The TV crews came and went and life carried on. The council screened the area off. The engineers moved in. Whatever they were doing didn't work. Now, the other side of The Sink is too distant to see without binoculars, except when it's really clear. Most days a haze hangs over it, cleared only occasionally by an updraught, and then, just for a moment, you can see the buildings on the other side, almost a mirror image of the structures around you. You can't help but imagine the people over there looking back from a place that doesn't even feel like it's part of the same city anymore.

Nothing seems familiar now. A-listers arrive by helicopter to eat at pop-up restaurants run by TV chefs, and tourists come to get drunk on the terraces. They throw beer cans into the abyss, trying to guess its depth. Sightseers take selfies among the broken remnants of disappearing neighbourhoods. At night, cars full of drunken kids burn rubber along deserted streets. From the safety of a viewing platform you can enjoy a cocktail and take in the panorama as the rocks and earth shiver and crumble away, exposing the arteries that fed the city. Water pipes and sewers spew their contents into the void, and torn power cables pop and spark. The ground erodes a little further each day and the platforms are drawn back in accordance with the updated government erosion projections.

◊

I get home from work, eat, and open a beer . . .

Actually, that's bullshit. I haven't been to work at all. The truth is, I lost my job after Jen left home. They gave me a written warning for absence and lack of diligence. I told them to stick it up their arse. It didn't matter anyway, that was a Friday and by Monday the office was gone. I could have stayed with the company when they relocated, but to be fair, I was never what you'd call a highly motivated employee. Since then I've been living on the relocation money. Every day, I get the bus to the outer suburbs and eat my lunch outside the offices of Greyson Bros. Ltd, where Jen has worked since her old company went down. I guess she knows, because she keeps out of sight. So there you go. Cheers.

I did see Jen a few days ago, but it wasn't at her work. It was pure luck, if you can call it that. I'd been drinking in a bar that had been a shoe shop on our local high street. Further along the road, the shops ended suddenly and beyond, where a city should have been, was blue sky. The truncated four-lane highway disappeared into a sea of market stalls and marquees. From a crowd across the street, she turned around, catching my eye for a second before walking on. She gave me nothing. Not even a smile. I watched until she disappeared into the crowd, then ducked into the doorway of a closed-up shop to compose myself. When I looked at my reflection in the storefront, I realised she hadn't recognised me. My hair and beard had grown chaotic, and my shirt was stained and stretched across my recently developed paunch.

When it gets dark, I put on a record and go out onto the porch with a couple of bottles of cheap red. I let the music play out, listening to the soft click and crackle of the needle on the turning disc and wonder why Jen went. Sipping the wine, I find myself thinking about the first night we slept together. She was still going out with some guy she'd met through work. I wanted her – I really wanted her – but I felt weird about it. I know, all's fair in love and war, and all that, but I had to bring it up.

'What about Martin?'

'He'll be okay.'

'You don't like him anymore?'

'Yes, I like him. Of course I do. But it's just . . . you know. Everyone likes Pot Noodles – what's that look for, food-snob? You love them too – Anyway, I like the chicken and mushroom flavour, but if I have it all the time, it gets boring.'

Not long after that, Martin was history.

◊

I wake on the sofa with a stiff neck and a headache. Before I open my eyes I realise I can smell the dog and a moment of unexpected happiness floods through me as I expect to feel his warm bulk squashed against me in my make-shift bed. Then I realise I've pulled the dog's old blanket around me in the chill of the early morning, and all at once, everything that has happened rushes back into me.

I sit up and push the window open. I'm still cold, but the air in the house is sour. Slouched over the back of the sofa, my head on the windowsill, I wait for the fresh air to revive me. I know it's Saturday because the guy across the street is out polishing his car. He sees me watching, gives me the finger, and goes back to the waxing. It's reassuring to see how we've all pulled together in the face of adversity.

I have let myself go. The house is a mess. I'm a mess. The relocation money is disappearing fast. I don't move from the sofa for a long time, but when I finally do, I have resolved to sort out my life. I do the laundry, clean the house, then I shower and make a long overdue trip to see Ray, my barber.

Ray stayed. There was no point in him moving on. Lung cancer will get him before anything else catches up with him. He smokes continually, a fag always burning in the ashtray, blue smog stinging your eyes as he works the scissors and comb. I wait for my turn in Ray's antique chair and watch him work. With each head, he uses a cutthroat for the final flourish, phlegm rattling in his throat as he steadies his shaking hand. A last adjustment to show them he's a perfectionist. Still proud, even though there's no point anymore.

◊

That night, I phone her. When she answers I can't bring myself to say anything. I listen to her breathing until she sighs and hangs up. Later, I call again. I'm feeling more confident – drunker anyway. I want to tell her that I've turned a corner, cleaned up, stopped drinking – more or less. I want to tell her I have a plan to get my old job back. I want to blurt all this out, but I can tell she isn't in the mood.

'I need to see you again. There's stuff I want to tell you,' I say.

'Tell me now.'

'Face to face, I mean . . .'

'I don't think that would be a good idea.'

'At least think about it. How about a coffee, somewhere neutral?' I immediately hate myself for using the word 'neutral'. It implies there's a conflict. Stupid. Stupid. Stupid.

'No.'

'I don't want it to be like this between us. What if The Sink is the end of everything?'

'Have you been looking at conspiracy websites again?'

As it happens, I have, but I choose to rise above this cheap shot. 'I keep dreaming that I was one of the ones who saw it open up and I didn't do anything.'

'Just move, for God's sake. Go to a different town like I did.'

'What do you mean, different town?' Whose office had I been sitting outside? 'I thought you worked at Greyson's and lived with Janine?'

'That was only for a couple of weeks, while I got my shit together. It wasn't easy for me either, Roy.'

'I know, I'm sorry. I don't want to move. This is our house.'

'Not anymore, Roy. I'm hanging up. I care about you. I do. But I want you to stop calling me,'

'Wait. How do you know the world isn't ending? This might be our last chance, if The Sink swallows everything.'

'I think they'd know.'

'Maybe they do and they're just not telling us.'

There's a long pause. I hear her sigh. 'If the world was ending, I think the queues at the post office would be longer. Go to bed, Roy. It's late.'

On a quiet night, you can hear a strange music from The Sink; long notes, rising and falling in pitch. They say it's the sound made by the wind pouring across its lip and plunging downwards, but it sounds like voices. Recently my dreams about The Sink have been different. I see the hole is full of water. Not a static pool, but a subterranean tide that surges and heaves beneath us, as though the whole world is only a brittle skin floating on a black ocean.

◊

I'm waiting for my old colleagues in a trendy vodka bar called The Holey Spirit. It's early afternoon, but people get here early to make the most of the views; there isn't much to see after dark. I'm here because, in order to impress Jennifer, I want to get my job back. This means kissing the arse of Alex – team leader and fucking idiot. My colleagues, though aware of my plan, have invited me out because they are – needlessly – worried about me, and they are trying to set me up with Marie, a friend of somebody in the office. Apparently, Marie is 'recovering from a broken heart', which, I point out, I am not.

As the afternoon goes on, we get drunker. I speak to Alex, but I can't force myself to bring up the job. He's such an anus. Eventually Nigel intercedes, shouting drunkenly, 'Hey, Lex, Roy wants his job back. Can he come back? It'll be great. Like the old days. Can he?' Alex says, 'No,' and more drinks arrive on the table.

One by one, my colleagues drop away until it is just me and Marie. It's still early, so she suggests a walk to sober us up. We head out into the crowds. You have to be careful in Holeside. The buildings left behind by the people and companies that have moved on now house a community of squatters, crims and weirdos. On the other hand, the ring of valueless real-estate has given birth to flea markets, galleries, artists' studios, music festivals and the ever-present ruin-bars. It has an energy that I don't remember the city ever having before. Marie is acting like it's the first time she's been here.

'I love the markets. You get some really cool stuff.'

'I don't come here much. I feel guilty that I'm getting stuff cheap because of someone else's misfortune.'

'What?'

'You know all the stuff on the markets is what the evacuees couldn't take with them, right?'

'Maybe you're helping them out, buying stuff they don't need.'

'It's commercialised now, anyway. None of it's real. They're all dealers offloading tat.'

'What about all the birds. You must love them.' She's talking about the gulls that are drawn here by all the crap being dumped over the edge. 'It's like being at the seaside.'

'Yeah, I suppose so.' I fucking hate seagulls.

We go to another bar and get beers and tapas. She says things like 'lusharama' when she tastes a new dish. We do some slammers, talk about work, and order cocktails. We're getting on OK until she looks at me with a caring frown and says, 'I hope you don't mind, but Stacey told me about Jennifer. She wasn't very nice to you.'

'Stacey or Jennifer?'

The place is getting busier with the evening crowd and the music has been turned up, so I don't hear her reply. I think I catch the word 'bitch'.

'Yeah, well, what the fuck do you know, Marie?' I don't think she can hear me either because she laughs and sucks on her straw.

◊

I don't remember coming home or falling asleep, but I wake on the couch again. It takes me a moment to realise someone is tapping loudly on the open window above me. With effort, I raise my head. It's Marie. I throw myself to the floor just as she looks through the window. I lie on the carpet for a few seconds, weighing my options. There is no way she didn't see me. I take a deep breath and get up.

'Hi.' She waves through the glass.

'Oh, hi, Marie.'

I am ill-prepared for conversation, but I pull the dog's blanket around my shoulders and open the door.

'You hiding?'

'No! God, no. You startled me. I fell out of bed. I never

sleep on the sofa. I must have nodded off or something . . .'

'I only came round to see if you were okay.'

'Okay.'

'I tried to call you, but I couldn't get through. I was worried.'

'Yeah, the phone masts have gone. The signal's not so great anymore.'

'Bummer. Fun though, not having a phone. Like the old days, when you actually had to talk to people instead of texting all the time.'

'Yeah.' I smile, but for me this is not a good thing.

'Anyway, so . . . I wanted to apologise. I didn't mean what I said. I was a bit drunk.'

I can't remember what she said. I have no idea what she is talking about.

'God, yeah. Me too.'

'What drunk or . . .?'

'Both. I was drunk too, but I'm sorry as well.'

She smiles. It seems to be the correct response. We talk for a bit until there is a long pause, and she says she should get going and leave me to my hangover. We hug and there is another pause.

'I'm glad we talked.'

'Me too.'

I wave her off from the porch. As she walks away I'm struck by how pretty she is. Part of me wishes she was staying, but I'm glad she's going because I'm so hungover I can't see straight. I'm about to call out, to ask if she's doing anything next weekend, when I have a sudden flashback of tearfully telling her that I'm a Pot Noodle. There was an argument too, its cause lost in a swirling blur of cocktail-induced vagueness. It would never work out between us.

◊

The edge is coming closer. They say there are cracks spreading out to the city limits. People work around them, fill the fissures, patch the concrete and fix the ruptured pipes and cables. The fugacious community of the hole's perimeter falls back and overnight our neighbourhood is busy again. There is noise, litter, and tourists' cars block the driveway at the weekends. It's not as bad as it could be – Holeside is more dissipated now, and there are more spectacular places to take in the view than our dull little patch. In other boroughs of the city, there are waterfalls where rivers pour out into nothing, turning to mist and rainbow long before they find the bottom. In other places, dissolving civic buildings, motorways and railways spawn rows of viewing platforms, bars and restaurants. All we have to offer here is the diminishing shell of the bus station and an ice-cream van.

The services are becoming erratic. There are frequent blackouts and, when another main breaks, the pressure drops and the water comes out brown. We work around it. In fact, it's difficult to remember what life was like before. Not just in respect of the practical things – I mean the less tangible stuff, like what the centre of the city used to look like. I struggle to recall the streets and boulevards we used to walk down in the days before Downtown disappeared. The shops, the cinemas, the town hall, train stations, the cathedral too, are all gone now, as if they had never existed.

All the time we spent there seems like a dream, as though, when the buildings and streets had gone, the memories became untethered and started to drift away, lost to us.

I have a photograph of Jen taken after we moved in together. We are with friends in a little Italian restaurant. It was in one of the narrow lanes in the old part of town, behind the cathedral. In the picture, we're all laughing, but I can't remember what we were laughing at, nor can I remember, other than in the vaguest terms, what the restaurant looked like or exactly which street it was in. It's all gone.

In the photos and videos we took, we are different people, but they are almost the only evidence I have that she was ever here. When she left, she took nearly everything with her. She bought most of it, so I suppose it's fair. She also took a lot of my records, which I feel less philosophical about. I have two of her jackets. When she left, she forgot to look in the back porch where they were hanging. I suppose she was too proud to come back for them, or embarrassed, or lazy, or whatever . . . So I still have them. I could post them, but if I can get her to collect them it's a chance for us to talk and work things out.

◊

Somehow, I never quite believed The Sink would actually get here. The houses at the end of the block are gone and the other end of the street has been cut off to traffic by a fissure three-feet wide. We cross it on a plank bridge to get to the market. The electricity has gone off, and there's a crack in the bathroom wall you can see daylight through.

Sink

Jen said she didn't want her jackets back. They were old ones that she didn't like anymore. I kept them for a few days, then I went to the end of the street where the Give Way sign that once marked the intersection with the main road leans out over nothing. I stood between a temporary viewing platform and an overflowing bin and threw them into The Sink. I'd been drinking and it seemed like a romantic gesture or something . . . I don't know.

◊

It's quiet here now. Rain is keeping the tourists away. The relocation money is spent, and I suppose I should move on. Even Mrs Meyers has gone. The last of us hold on to these little patches of life, preserving what we had, and lingering, hoping that, in the face of our collective will, time will stand still. At night I lie awake and, from somewhere in the darkness outside, comes the sound of softly tumbling masonry and soil. As more of the world vanishes, I listen, holding my breath, wishing the dog would come back, and hoping Jen will.

The Killing Tree

I F THE JUDGE finds them guilty, they are brought here, to the killing tree. When I first came here, I thought the tree would be huge, black, and hung with the bodies of wrongdoers, but it is just this, twisted and stunted by thirst. The tree itself is a miracle of survival; the only one for many miles. It is my only company out here where the town is just a smoky bruise on the horizon.

I take pride in what I do. If they are not buried deep, hyenas will get them. A professional knows this. There is skill in digging a good hole in this ground. The red earth has many stones and it crumbles easily. There is a knack also in getting out of the grave once it is dug – especially for an old man like me. One day it will be a permanent stay, I think. I dig the graves away from the tree and this suits us both; I don't have to hack through its old roots and the tree suffers no damage.

When I was young, I would watch the trials. Watch the prisoner plead for forgiveness and then watch the family loudly demanding compensation for their loss. It's no good.

Nobody here has money, not even to buy their life. So, they bring them here and tie them to the tree. The guards give the family the gun. It is an old AK47. Its wooden stock is worn from handling. It is loaded with five bullets. The family are permitted five shots.

The tree has many bullet holes.

Over the many years I have done this job, I have noticed something: when it's done, they never look at each other, and they always hurry away.

Heaven

WEEKENDS ALWAYS END like this. Her sucking him off in his van before she goes inside to do her homework. Today, unflatteringly, he seems distracted.

'Wait. There's somebody watching us . . .Seriously. Stop. Look.'

She sits up, wipes her mouth, re-buttons her top and looks around.

In the caravan next to the one she shares with her mother, Chrissy sees movement in the gloom behind the net curtains.

'Just Old Annie. She's been keeping an eye out for me since the thing with Toby,' she says.

'Has he been acting up again?'

'No. You scared him.'

'I'll maim the fat fuck if he comes near you.'

'My hero.'

'I mean it.'

'Just leave it. I'm fed up with thinking about him and his stupid fucking dog.'

Arron looks back towards Annie's window. 'She was watching us last week too.'

'Maybe she fancies you.'

She fixes her hair up where it's fallen loose. While she's cleaning herself up and re-applying lipstick, Arron's talking. As usual, most of what he says is just noise for the sake of it, so she stops listening. Soon he will leave and she will spend the evening at the table in the caravan's cramped kitchen, studying for her re-sits and wondering what the girls she'd known at school are doing. They kiss goodbye and she crosses the parking area, gravel crunching underfoot. He shouts after her, asks if she's missing him already. She laughs and gives him the finger as he reverses back down the path.

Searching in her bag for the door key, her smile fades suddenly; from the corner of her eye she can see Toby watching from his decking. She's not worried, not exactly; he hasn't come anywhere near her since Arron threatened him. He got right in Toby's face, said he'd kill him if he even looked at her again, everybody watching by then, peeping around curtains or poking their heads out of their front doors to see what the shouting was about, hoping it would turn nasty and the police would come again. Eventually things calmed down and she thought it was all done and dusted, but later Toby told everyone it was Chrissy who killed his dog.

She tried to tell him that it was a mistake; she was just in the wrong place at the wrong time. She'd been leaving for college when she saw him behind his 'van. She knew something was wrong. He was looking down at where the dog was lying on the floor, except that she didn't know then that it was the dog, or what had happened. Toby had one hand pressed against the side of his trailer supporting himself and she could see the thin metal buckling slightly under his weight. He looked hung-over, face white, sweating, head hanging heavily down to his chest. 'I thought he was barfing,' she told people later; not unusual for him, after all. Thinking he'd been drinking all night, she'd laughed at him and said, 'That'll teach you.' Only when he'd turned towards her did she see he was crying. He stared at her coldly for a long time, then went quietly indoors. Embarrassed and unsure what to do, she went on her way. That evening, when she got back from college, it all kicked off, him banging on the side of their caravan, screaming blue murder.

'Jesus, it wasn't me. Why would I?' Most of the onlookers had gone by then. Only her mother, a couple of the park's other residents, and Annie still lingered in the parking area between the caravans. 'I don't even get what he's so upset about. He hated it. Always shouting at the fucking thing and kicking it around.' The dog had chewed through its rope and escaped half-a-dozen times. Each time it came back. It probably died out of stupidity, she thought. Later, to her horror, her mother offered to pay for the dog's cremation. Chrissy knew she wasn't serious; she could barely cover the bills and put petrol in the car. Even so, it made things worse. It was clear to everyone that even she thought Chrissy had done it.

Her mother, Jean, has the same eyes and mouth as Chrissy, even the same hair. From a distance they could be twin sisters. Sometimes Chrissy finds this comforting, sometimes it frightens her. She is afraid of being like her mother; afraid of getting old and being stuck in a place like this, singing along to Juice Newton and John Denver while she's doing the housework. Jean says her voice used to be like Chrissy's, but cigarettes and the passing of time have left their mark and her range isn't what it was. She likes to tell stories of when she sang in clubs, back in the days when Chrissy's father was still around. He's been gone a long time and since he left Jean has worked hard to keep their heads above water. The child maintenance payments never arrived. Jean maintains hopeful contact with a solicitor, but Chrissy's nearly eighteen now and neither of them are expecting a cheque for back payments any time soon.

It's just the two of them now, but Chrissy had a brother once. He died cleaning out a petrochemical tank when an unidentified co-worker turned off the air supply to his suit. There was an inquiry, but they never figured out if it was a prank gone wrong or just an accident. People closed ranks, stories were straightened out, procedures were tightened. Chrissy misses him, but sometimes she can hardly remember what he looked like. Four years is a long time.

They live at the back of the park, where their caravan – along with those occupied by Annie and Toby – is part of a small cluster sited in the crescent of an old quarry. This is the end of the park that's farthest from the sea, and farthest from civilisation; the Wild West. It is out of sight of the main park and the 'vans here are older; reconditioned and bought for a song. The lawns aren't mowed and hedges hide tips of garden waste crowned with the rusting frames of deckchairs and broken swing sets. None of the rules are quite as strictly enforced here as they are elsewhere on the site. Pam, the manager, doesn't mind as long as no one else can see, and as long as she gets her money.

Unsettled by Toby's staring at her, Chrissy abandons her search for the door keys and, as she often does when she wants to be alone, climbs the fence and walks around the edge of the park to the top of the quarry. From there she can see the sea and, in the other direction, the distant outline of the city stalking along the horizon. Below her, a wave of uncut grass and bramble thickets pushes against the rock face and the 'vans look like boats hauled up along a shoreline; boats that never go anywhere.

Across the hotchpotch of metal roofs and satellite dishes, and past the ordered world of freshly glossed fences and the rows of new 'vans where the holiday makers stay, is a nightclub with a bar, a dance floor, and a stage where comedians and bands perform, working the coastal circuit in summer. Beside it is a kids' indoor play area and the Cheeky Monkeys club where Chrissy works in the holidays. The money is okay, but she doesn't like it. Arron told her once that he wouldn't mind if they had a baby. She thought about her Morning Monkeys group and told him she'd rather burst her own eyeball.

◊

After dinner Chrissy and Jean fight, again.

Depending on what day of the week it is, Jean thinks Arron is either too poor to be worthy of her daughter, too stupid to be any use, or just too old: 'He's closer to my age than yours,' she snaps at Chrissy. Chrissy knows this is not true and thinks her mother is jealous. Before Arron there was another guy, Neil. It had ended badly and Jean came out one morning to find 'I love u' scratched into the paintwork of her car. Chrissy knew it was Neil straight away. He thought it was her car. When she started seeing him, she'd told him it was hers to impress him and never seemed to find the opportunity to tell him the truth. Even so, it was the words themselves that gave him away; the letters he'd scratched into the bonnet were small, sorry for their own existence, like him. Jean was livid, but Chrissy sensed excitement too, until she found out the message was meant for Chrissy, not her, then she was just livid. Jean still drove her to college though. On the twenty-minute drive, both sat in silence looking out across the scratched bonnet. All the way Chrissy wondered if it had been the prospect of Neil, specifically, being in love with her that Jean had found exciting, or just the idea that someone had been in love with her again after so long.

Although, as usual, it is the subject of Arron that provides the flash point, it is not him that is troubling Jean. It is her daughter's desire to leave. The cold-hearted singlemindedness with which Chrissy has pursued this aim over the last twelve months terrifies her. Jean isn't sure when this fear began, but it's been there a long time, growing quietly. Years ago, when Chrissy was only a girl, she noticed her watching plane trails crossing the sky. The city's airport wasn't far away and planes regularly circled in a holding pattern above the house they lived in.

'What you lookin' at, Chrissybabes?'

'Planes,' she replied. 'I'm gonna fly in them, when I'm grown up.'

'Is that right? You gonna be a stewardess?'

'No. I'm gonna be a businesswoman.' Jean knew she didn't know what a businesswoman was – she'd seen pictures in one of her magazines: rich women travelling first class; the people the stewardesses waited on. It shouldn't have meant anything, but Jean thought of it every time she watched Chrissy tracking a plane across the sky.

'You don't wanna go off somewhere, do you?'

'Yeah, course I do.'

Since then, Chrissy has worked hard. Any other mother, she thinks guiltily, would be proud. If it hadn't been for the bad patch after her brother died, Chrissy would have her qualifications by now.

The prospect of being left alone keeps Jean awake at night. It gnaws at her. Some days, especially those when her daughter seems suddenly grown up – almost a stranger living under her roof – she is unable to let it lie.

'But you've got a good job at the club. You could probably get more hours once you've got college out of your system. Just think about it. That's all I'm asking.'

'I never do anything but bloody think, do I? There's fuck all else to do around here.'

'Stop moaning. When I was your age I was working all hours.'

'Yeah, well life was tough in the stone age, weren't it.'

'You watch your lip.'

'I hate it here. Everybody's always sticking their nose in. You can't breathe without somebody having a say about it.' There is a long silence. Toby's dog might as well be lying across the table between them, head lolling. 'People round here are just . . . I don't know. I don't want to stay here.'

'What, and you think you're so different from the rest of us, do you?'

'Maybe I am. I'll never find out at this rate, will I? I didn't even mean you anyway. Fucks' sake.'

'Watch your language.'

Out of habit Chrissy apologises and hates herself for it immediately. She grabs her college bag. The plates stacked in the sink rattle as she slams the door on her way out.

Out in the evening air, she starts to feel better. She hopes the laundrette near the park offices will still be open. It's nothing special but it's somewhere to go, and there's a drinks machine so she can get a coffee and sit on one of the benches with her Business Studies revision. When she reaches the mini-roundabout at the centre of the park, she can see that the laundrette is closed so she keeps going, reaching the park entrance and turning towards the village's main street – the village's only street. In readiness for the start of the holiday season, the sign on the main road has been re-painted with the words 'Sunny Haven Caravan Park' set against a powder-blue sky and golden-yellow beach. She hasn't looked at the sign in years and, like the other permanent residents, she has never called the park by its name. To them – and especially to the old-timers – it is Heaven; a reference to the old Methodist chapel next door. The chapel is a pound-shop now, with buckets and spades, toys and inflatables hanging outside.

It's late spring and the days are getting longer, but a cool north-easterly breeze is still coming in from the sea, carrying gritty sand and curls of dry seaweed along the street. She drinks in the bright colours of shop fronts, garishly painted neon boards advertising shops, the flashing lights of the empty amusement arcade and its jangling music.

Beyond the tattoo parlour and The Royal Dragoon where children are sliding down the tail of a fibreglass dinosaur in the beer garden, lie the concrete seawall and the shoreline. Nobody she knows goes to the beach. It's used by day trippers and the rich townies who own the huts further along. By day, Lycra-clad, alone, or in packs, they run and cycle along the front, or practice tai-chi in the dunes, but this evening Chrissy has the whole place to herself.

In a shelter on the deserted seafront, she stares at her revision book. Her frustration has subsided, but she still can't concentrate. When the sun dips below the buildings behind her she shivers but stays put. She wants Arron to come and get her, but she knows he won't. He'll be at home, asleep, with the alarm set to wake him for his night shift at the factory.

He promised her once that they'd leave together. As soon as he had the money they would drive away for good. She knows that he won't keep his promise, he's full of shit, and maybe, one day soon, she'll find he's gone without her. She doesn't really care. She doesn't love Arron, but she does like him. He's kind, most of the time, and he has a van. Wheels are important here; they stop you feeling like you can't escape. Plus, the factory where he works pays well, so at weekends he drives her to the city and takes her places. Anyway, she thinks, maybe it'll be her that leaves him behind and he'll become one of the old, fat guys in the Dragoon who never went anywhere or did anything but sit there talking as if they know it all. In fact, she smiles to herself, if he doesn't leave with her, that's exactly what he's got coming, sure as shit stinks.

It's Annie who finds her.

'What you so upset about then?'

'I'm not upset.'

'No, you don't look it neither. That's why you're sat out here on your own with a face like a smacked arse.'

Chrissy is pretty sure her face looks normal. 'Well, I ain't.'

'What is it, men troubles?'

'No.'

'How is he then, your fella? Going okay is it?'

You should know, Chrissy thinks. You're always watching us. 'We're okay,' she says. 'It's not him. It's Mum.'

'I knew there was something up. Come on. You can't stay out here all night'

When the thing with Toby's dog happened, Annie was the only one who stood up for her. When Toby had accused Chrissy, before Arron had arrived and warned him off, Annie intervened, told him to wind his fat neck in and stop saying things he couldn't prove. It had worked. Toby recoiled from her wagging finger and slunk back to his caravan. All the same, the next day he'd cornered her on her way back from the shop.

'I'm gonna fuck you up for what you did,' he said. His voice was soft, claggy, as though he had a mouth full of wet cloth. 'And your mum too.'

'I told you, it wasn't me who fucking done it.' Her voice sounded weak, high pitched. Over the dome of Toby's obesely rounded shoulder, she could see the cluster of caravans where they lived and it seemed impossibly far away.

'Yeah, well who was it then, you cunt?'

For a moment she wanted to cry, but not from fear. It was the sudden and misplaced feeling of loneliness, of abandonment by the people who might have protected her – Arron and her mother, her father, even her brother. It wasn't only that making her breath catch at the back of her throat, it was frustration too; anger at the unfairness of the accusation and her powerlessness to prove her innocence.

Once again, it had been Annie who came to her rescue. Toby and Chrissy became aware of her standing on her doorstep, staring at them. Annie said nothing, but Toby was rattled.

'What's it gotta do with you?' he mumbled, already moving off in the direction of The Dragoon. 'Nosy old slag.'

Annie's cold gaze followed him until he was out of sight, then she calmly went inside and closed her door.

Jean disliked Annie, though Chrissy was never sure why. When Chrissy told her about Annie's intervention, instead of being grateful as Chrissy had expected, Jean had snapped,

'Don't you go paying any attention to that daft old bat.'

'She's the only one who stuck up for me.'

'She's just a lonely old woman.'

'Fucks that supposed to mean?'

'It means she's probably lonely for a good reason.'

'Like what?'

'Like she's a not-right. They don't take your kids away for nothing, always out on the sauce, or with fellas.'

'Oh yeah, and when was that supposed to 've happened? She's about a hundred and ninety.'

'I'm just saying, she ain't exactly a saint.'

'What and you are, I suppose?'

'Don't be stupid, Chrissy. At least I never left you alone so I could go out and get rat-arsed.'

'Yeah, well at least she was on my side.'

The clatter and crash of the seafront minimarket closing its shutters jolts Chrissy from her thoughts. Annie has said something and is looking at her expectantly. She is waiting for the answer to a question that Chrissy, tired and distracted, her mind elsewhere, hasn't taken in. She looks worried but lets it go. 'Come on, let's get you a cuppa.'

◊

In Annie's kitchenette, Chrissy can't think of anything to say and for a long time the only sounds are the soft chirruping of Annie's budgerigar and the hiss of the gas jets beneath the kettle. The space is a mirror image of her own caravan, with the familiar smell of cooking and bottled gas, but less choked with the detritus of daily life, almost spartan. Annie raises a comforting hand to Chrissy's face. 'You're frozen.'

'Forgot my jacket, din I.'

'So what's going on with your mum, then?'

'She wants me to stay here forever.'

'And what do you want, darlin'? You wanna get going and see a bit of the world?'

'Yeah. She don't care though, does she.'

'I'm sure that ain't true. She'll miss you if you go, that's all. Everyone will.'

'Yeah right. She just hates being on her own. And who else will miss me? Everyone here hates me.'

'Don't you take no notice of Toby and those other idiots.'

'Won't matter soon. I'm getting out of here, soon as I've done my exams.'

'Here you go, darlin', drink this. You want sugar?' Chrissy takes one and stirs her mug. They stand close together, sipping the hot tea. 'You still at college?'

'Yeah. Still.'

'Well, it's not forever. You got all the time in the world.'

Chrissy thinks about the people on her course; all returners, people who fucked up their lives, got made redundant, got pregnant, whatever, and have gone back to try again. They are old. After her, the next youngest is twenty-nine; twenty-nine and still going to college. She does not have all the time in the world.

'Yeah, well I don't fancy working in The Dragoon for the next ten years.'

'What you gonna do?'

'S'pose it depends on my grades.'

'What'll we do without you?' Annie chuckles. 'And what about Andy?'

'Arron.'

'Yeah. What about him?' Chrissy notices something about the way Annie says *him,* a hint of suspicion, dislike even. 'He going with you?'

Chrissy shrugs. Suddenly she feels defensive of Aaron, and the thought of moving to the city alone, without him, seems impossible. 'Maybe. I'll see if he wants to come.'

'Well, you watch out. Men are no good. Only one thing on their minds and once they've got it they're off. Trust me. I was young once. I know what they're like. Men are all animals, sweetheart. Pretty thing like you, gotta be careful.'

Chrissy doesn't want to talk about Aaron, or men at all, but finds herself thinking about Mr Crabb, her old history teacher. He'd tried to persuade her to apply for university. She liked him until she caught him looking up her skirt. She'd thought she was imagining it, but when he realised she was staring back at him he had flushed a deep, embarrassed pink. Did that make him an animal? She didn't hate him for it, it just put her off doing history. Neither can she imagine her brother ever behaved like an animal; he was always kind to everyone. Then she thinks of Arron and how, after he's come, he looks at her as though he's done her a favour.

Annie breaks the silence. 'Oh well, it don't matter anyway. The world's your oyster. You're young and clever. Too clever for this place.'

For the second time that evening, Annie gently touches Chrissy's cheek. Her fingers tremble and Chrissy wonders if she's nervous or is that just what happens when you get old? Maybe it's something else; she is acting strangely, her movements and her words seem mismatched, and her expression hard to read. Then something occurs to Chrissy.

'You think it was me too, don't you?'

'What, darlin'?'

'Toby's dog.'

Annie recoils. 'No! Of course I don't.'

'You do. I can tell you do.'

'I know it wasn't you.'

'How? How do you know?'

Annie pauses, then quietly says, 'Coz it was me what done it.'

'You?'

Annie nods.

'But why? Why would you hurt his dog? Jesus. It had enough problems livin' with 'im.'

'Exactly! He made that dog's life a fuckin' misery. I had a front-row seat to everything he did.' Annie nods towards the window that looks out towards Toby's little yard. 'Every bloody night, it felt like. I had to do something and I couldn't poison that fat bastard, could I? They'd have put me in prison. At least it ain't sufferin' anymore.'

'But you let them go on thinking it was me. They all think it was me, even Mum.'

'I'm so sorry, sweetheart. How could I have known they'd think it was you what done it. I never thought for a minute it would come back on you.'

'You gonna tell them then?'

Annie looks pale. 'Why? What they think and what they can prove is two different things, ain' it. As long as they don't know who done it, they can't do nothing about it.'

'They aren't threatening you though, are they?'

'They won't do nothing. They're all mouth.'

'Easy for you to say.'

'Well, what's done is done, and forgotten is as good as mended.'

◊

Around the park, yellow light filters through curtains and blinds, and doors are shut and locked. Apart from the distant shouts of some kids messing about, the only sounds come from the seagulls wheeling in the violet-tinged darkness above. Chrissy doesn't want to go home – can't face it – not yet, so she walks for a while.

In the wilderness at the edge of the park, a thicket of brambles grows in front of the old quarry face. Later in the year, on sticky summer evenings, glow worms fill it with blue-white beads of light. It's the females that glow. They shine brighter when she watches them from the corner of her eye, as though they're shy and can feel her gaze. Those pin-pricks of light, glowing together in the darkness, make her feel part of something bigger and more beautiful. Tonight she needs them, but they're not there. It's still too cold, too early in the year.

When she gets back to her own caravan, she goes to bed without speaking to her mother. Through the thin wall she hears voices on the TV and then a moment of quiet followed by the sound of the remote control being dropped onto the coffee table and a wine glass being placed in the sink.

Before her mother turns off the lights and goes to bed, she checks in on Chrissy, kissing the top of her head and closing the door behind her. Chrissy takes out her college notepad and begins to write. In the weak glow of her nightlight, the pen bites into the paper. She writes quickly, angrily, and in places the words are almost illegible, but it will do. She barely sleeps that night. A nervous energy fills her, making her hot and cold at the same time. In the morning she posts the note into Toby's mailbox at the site office.

That evening, after college, Chrissy lies in her bedroom watching the blue lights flicker through her curtain. Her window is open and the air carries the chatter of police radios and the hushed voices of the paramedics outside Annie's caravan.

The Unmaking

T HINGS ARE SHARPER here: colours; light. The sky and sea are brilliant blue. The meeting of water and air is a precise line that stretches across the horizon. Even after the storm of the previous night, the beach is uncluttered by seaweed or flotsam. Behind the beach there are palm trees and thick undergrowth. It is a child's drawing rendered in bright colours.

A man and a woman walk hand in hand along the shore, leaving footprints in a meandering line. Both are in their early twenties. The man is tall, almost handsome, wearing a pale yellow shirt and faded cargo shorts. The woman is dark haired, tanned, much shorter and taking four quick steps for every three of his. Christian is an Englishman – a drifting graduate with a second-class degree. Tegan, a New Zealander, is the daughter of a surgeon, taking a year out before starting an internship with an architecture practice in Melbourne. The slack swing of his arms and his long stride make her compact presence seem more energetic.

They met on a beach. Not this one. It was on the cool, windswept sands north of Hokitika, at a party thrown by disparate groups of backpackers from local hostels. The flames of a huge driftwood bonfire were whipped by the wind and beyond its light a constellation of smaller fires and barbecues glowed in the darkness. Christian drifted between the groups for a while, recognising faces from the hostels, bus terminals and tourist attractions along the backpacking routes.

The evening turned to night and the party unfolded just as he might have expected. Campervans lined the beach road. The poster in town said, 'bring your own booze and food', so bags of supermarket beer lay everywhere, half-buried in the sand. A guy with an acoustic guitar sang inappropriately sad songs to a group of bored girls until he was drowned out by loud reggae and some drunken Canadians limbo dancing under a plank of driftwood.

He was thinking of leaving when he saw her face in the firelight. She joked about his accent. He loved hers, and the way his name sounded when she said it. In the darkness below the dunes, the tide rose until they could feel the breakers shaking the sand. They stayed until dawn, watching the fire burn down and the lights of Hokitika dwindle as the sky grew lighter. Over the five weeks since their first fireside meeting, they haven't been apart.

They don't recognise the whale for what it is until they are almost close enough to touch it. With the sun in their eyes, it seems to be nothing more than a rock formation projecting from the shallows. It is lying in two feet of water, half its face and one flank above the lapping waves, its upturned eye is glazed, unmoving. It is only a small species, or perhaps a juvenile, but still large enough to distort under its own weight. Although the creature is motionless, they are afraid to approach it. Even as dead weight, the unexpected proximity of something so large is intimidating. It is she who is the first to move cautiously towards it.

'Is it alive?'

'I don't think so. It must have come ashore in the storm.'

'Maybe.' Even though there can be no other explanation, she doesn't sound convinced.

In the water around the creature, a trace of blood tints the shallows hinting at trauma, but they can see no injuries. Although neither speaks of it, they are both thinking of the whales they had seen from the back of a tourist boat off the coast of Kaikora, where dozens of tourist cameras pointed towards the slow rise and dive, waiting for the lunge downwards, hoping for the flick of a tail. But those whales, impressive as they had been, were a distant spectacle. This stranded creature, though much smaller, is more real, more impressive than any of those they had seen out at sea.

He wades into the water and carefully reaches out and touches the creature's skin. He puts his ear to the whale's flank listening for signs of life. He can hear nothing over the sploshing of the waves around them. He hadn't expected to. 'I just want to see if it's breathing,' he tells her, because pressing his face to the grey flank seems like an act of intimacy that somehow needs to be excused; to touch something so rare, so massive, from a world completely alien to his own, requires a reason.

He senses rather than sees a movement. Was it the motion of the water, the swell pushing the creature's fins? And then, taking him off guard and causing him to fling himself backwards, the creatures breathes: a single rasp from the blowhole, like the choking start of a word.

'Fuck. It's alive.'

'You reckon?'

He's irritated by her sarcasm. 'Well, we've got to help it.'

'How?'

Out here, two miles from town, it's a reasonable question.

They try to push it out into deeper water, hands pressing into the whale's smooth body, the creature's muscles yielding under the pressure. When pushing fails, they try dragging it by its tail.

'It's no good. We can't move it like this. We're just going to hurt it.'

Both of them have phones, but neither has a signal. For a moment they stand helpless, each staring at the arc of the creature's side, like polished stone. It is drying out, burning, barely holding onto life. They take spare clothes and their towels and soak them, covering as much of the whale as they can, draping the soaked cloth over its head and splashing water across its skin to beat the killing sun. Tegan stops abruptly. 'This is just pointless. We're just postponing the inevitable.'

'We can't just let it die. One of us will have to go for help.'

'Me. I'm faster.'

Christian hesitates, unsure if he wants to be left as the whale's sole guardian.

'Okay. Tell them . . .'

'What?'

'Tell them to bring buckets and ropes . . . and a tractor.'

'Thanks. I wouldn't have thought of that.'

Her acidity, and her apparent eagerness to leave, are remnants of the previous night's tension. Something they had talked out, agreed was done with, but still lies just below the surface.

Christian keeps splashing water over the whale as he watches Tegan jogging away from him. Once she is out of sight, he pauses to catch his breath and the quiet closes in around him. It is the first time he has felt alone since he met her. Squinting against the light, he thinks to drape his shirt around the whale's eye, to keep off the worst of the light. 'Sorry.' In its eye he sees a reflection of himself in miniature, dark against the glare of the sky. Staring into its bottomless deep, he feels empty, unbalanced.

His thoughts drift back to their arrival on the island. Weary and hot, they had their first argument at the airport. Tired bickering that started with a lost pair of sunglasses – not even lost, just misplaced – escalated, fuelled by heat, boredom and the need for sleep. They booked an over-priced beach hut from a pushy guy in the arrivals hall and took a taxi.

Neither of them spoke during the journey. In the silence, he watched the taxi driver's glances in the mirror. The man assessed the foreigners wedged into the back seat of his tiny Fiat with a flat gaze, perhaps wondering why they weren't babbling excitedly about their holiday. He couldn't know that, for his passengers, the last six months had been a blur of islands, beach clubs, quaint harbours and tourist attractions. He talked to them about the sun, the beach, drinking rum—the things tourists like them enjoyed—until he sensed defeat and left them in silence. Christian wilted, drawing back into his seat, embarrassed by their failure to fulfil their role.

Their hut was one of a cluster on the beach, beyond the edge of town. It was beautiful but felt tainted by the hard sell at the airport and their early capitulation over the price. The aftershocks of the argument skulked on into the slow evening. Later, they picked at the food they had brought back from the buffet where they had endured a display of traditional dancing and drank too much of the local spirit. When they tried to sleep, the sound of people partying on the beach taunted them through the thin walls of the bungalow. It wasn't the noise that kept them awake, but the gnawing feeling that they should be out there too, that they were missing something. He left the sleeping space and moved out to a lounger, where he lay watching the sparse lights of town through the insect screens and listening to the hum of the refrigerator and ceiling fan blending with the gentle rush of waves outside.

When at last he slept, he dreamt of a bus journey in the rain; a dark morning surrounded by commuters, the air thickly damp and the windows opaque with mist. This other self, lulled to sleep by the gentle rocking of the bus, dreamt in turn of a perfect beach on a faraway island, its sands washed with sunlight and the waters of a crystal-blue ocean.

In the morning, the wake of their argument had dissipated, but the calm was still newly formed and fragile around them. Although he won't admit it to Tegan, he feels restless. This – they – will all be over soon. Their lives will call them to different hemispheres, and this knowledge fills him with a malaise that crawls over him like the breath of the British winter waiting for him over the horizon. He has already decided that he will not bring it up, and he is as certain as he can be that Tegan won't either.

The whale's tail curls upwards out of the water in a single weary flap, as though it is in pain or making a futile effort to move. Although this is the clearest sign of life it has given so far, the tension in the tail's compact muscle seems closer to rigor mortis than strength.

Tegan must be back at the town by now. How long had it taken them to walk here? Forty-five minutes? An hour? And they had dawdled, so she could be back in town in thirty minutes, twenty if she ran, and return with help in an hour or so. Say, an hour and a half if they needed to grab equipment – they were hardly likely to have a whale rescue kit easily to hand. Would they know from instinct or experience what was needed?

He keeps splashing, but he is flagging now, unused to labouring under a hot sun. His back aches from scooping, so he kneels and thrashes water messily over the creature's back and face. From here he is almost level with the gelatinous eye. It is blank, alien, but this time he thinks he sees something there: an acknowledgement? A connection? Perhaps what he sees is fear – his efforts giving fright rather than comfort.

He slows his actions a little, running water over its face as gently as he can, trying to wash away the sand around the eyes and mouth – it looks uncomfortable – but as the water runs away it leaves another sheen of tiny glittering grains which collect once again in the whale's eyes and the parted gap of its mouth. Tiring, he slumps next to it. For a moment he leans against the smooth grey bulk, then snaps himself upright, ashamed that he has used the dying creature for support.

Sitting in the shallows beside his companion, he feels the heave of the water around them and for a moment he feels weightless. He imagines the whale's yearning to be free from the gravity clamping it to the surface of his world, to sink through the bright silver membrane of the sea's surface, back into the twilight of its own world. He turns back to the body beside him as its tail rises from the shallow water and falls stiffly back again. Tegan will be back soon, he is sure.

He moves quickly again, throwing water as fast as he can over its face and back. His frenzied splashing seems ridiculous against the stillness of his patient. Scooping water in lunging swings, he stares down the long, empty beach. 'I should have gone myself,' he tells it softly. He carries on talking to the whale as though words mean something and will help, resigned now to keeping it company as it slips away from him. Watching him, the pool of blackness at the centre of its eye whispers back, 'You promised. You promised.'

He slumps against its flank again, placing his hands against the smooth skin, feeling that the life beneath it is fading. Then, down the beach, he sees a group of men, ten or more, carrying ropes and buckets and other equipment. He blinks the sweat out of his eyes to be sure before he tells it, 'Hang on, they're coming.' Hopeful once more, he starts splashing again, but slower now; exhaustion yielding to the knowledge that rescue is coming. Soon the animal will be someone else's responsibility. He feels both relief and regret at this prospect; it will no longer need him. He will go back to his part of the world and the whale will return to its depths.

The men are almost here, now. As they approach, their pace quickens, perhaps sensing the urgency of the situation. But, as they draw closer, Christian can see that what he had taken to be lifting tackle and shovels are nets and curved blades mounted on sticks. Breath held, Christian rests his hands gently on the whale's head. The men arrive so quickly that he is still like this when they surround him, smiling broadly, happy, shouting in their own language, patting him on the back.

For a moment they run their hands across the flanks of the whale, just as he had done when they had first found it, in awe of its size and beauty. They respectfully remove the towels and clothing draped across the beast's back and hand them to him. A rush of air escapes the whale's blowhole. Then the slicing begins. Before he realises what is happening the blades are cutting through the skin, into the muscle and blubber below, spilling blood and fibrous gobbets of yellow fat into the sand. He starts to speak, to protest, but instinctively understands that anything he could say would be met with misapprehension, ridicule, or perhaps even anger. There is nothing to be done. Any action he takes now will prolong the pain, so he hovers, inactive, on the edge of the group. Better it's over quickly. He watches because he cannot make himself look away. Despite the sun, a sickening coldness rises from somewhere inside him and, for a moment, he blames Tegan; she was the one who found these men and brought them here.

The blades seem hardly to meet the skin of the whale before it opens. He is surprised how easily the tough hide of the beast splits, as though something inside is pressing to get out: viscera, pink and wet, longing to escape the dark interior, eager to break out into the light, and tumble, liberated into the sunlit shallows. He fights an urge to wash the sand from the innards, as though he could make them clean again, put the creature back together, reverse its terrible unmaking.

After the first incisions it is a free for all, the older men pointing, giving instructions to the youngsters, each taking what he can. Christian stands knee deep in the water, watching the butchery as a flood of bright blood colours the water around them. The men are grateful, joking with him as they work. He smiles dumbly when, laughing, they offer him the penis – 'It is the most valuable part.'

When he carries his belongings up the beach to the dry sand, Tegan is nowhere to be seen. She hadn't arrived with the men as he'd expected, but far down the beach he sees a figure that might be her standing on a low bank of sand. The figure turns and walks slowly away, disappearing around the distant headland towards town.

Walking back along the beach, he crosses trails of tainted water from the fishermen's shacks concealed in the thick undergrowth behind the beach, staining the sand brown and grey. The thin lines of smoke rising from the cooking stoves are the only visible signs of the houses. On their walk out that morning, he hadn't noticed the streaks of filth in the sand. He looks away now, out to the unbroken blues of sea and sky. Later, in the bungalow, neither of them will mention what happened. It will be one more thing between them that will remain unspoken.

One day, years later, bored and staring from the window of his office into the rain-soaked car park outside, he will remember the whale and his attempt to save it, but it will be a shifting blur of sensations and images that he could just as easily have dreamt or seen in a film. He will think about Tegan too, trying unsuccessfully to remember what it was they had fought about and why they had gone their separate ways. He will recall their time together as a collage of movement and light, and glimpsed places: beaches, airports, backpacks and taxis, cheap hotels, and a hot, beachfront bungalow. Like the whale, all these moments will seem like faded postcards from another life. Mostly, he will remember her face in the firelight on a beach at midnight, and how he loved her accent and the way she said his name.

Stay

THE SUN HAS fallen behind the ridge, and below him most of the valley is in shadow. If he doesn't find the dog before dark, he'll have to give up. Hollins jogs across the open ground but can't keep it up. The turf is wet and uneven and he stumbles frequently as he goes, scanning the gills around him for any sign of the animal. The blood in his hand pumps against the dog's lead, wound tightly around his fingers.

He'd promised Helen it wouldn't get out again. She never liked him keeping the dog in the shed: 'It's not used to being out there.' But it needs to learn its place. It's never done as it's told, never been any good as a working dog. The boy had spoiled it with kindness. It's like him, always has to be off somewhere, any chance it gets to slip loose. He should've drowned the bloody thing on the day it was abandoned to their care.

Helen speaks about the dog as though their boy will be back one day to collect it, and there is always accusation in her voice: 'You're too hard on it. It's not a farm dog. Don't you ever learn? You leave it in that shed and it'll get out again. You mark my words, it'll go looking.' Whenever she speaks about the dog, there is always the whisper of something bigger underneath.

After the boy went, there were weeks of shouted words that Hollins can only half remember now; memory obliterated by the white noise of anger. Six months later the police came to the door. A man and a woman, both young, both smart: 'Mr Hollins? Do you mind if we come in?' All the time they were there the dog had skulked in the kitchen doorway, as though it knew. After that, the fighting gave way to long silences.

She'll be home from work by now, in the kitchen of the farmhouse, with its smell of sour bacon fat and dust gathering slowly in corners. They still call it the farmhouse, though it hasn't been a farm for a long time. She'll think the dog is with him, out on the fell.

From the garden gate, he saw it bolt down the lane; a flash of black and white. He knows it came this way, but it is impossible to tell which direction it's gone. He guesses it would follow a route it remembers, the way it used to go with the boy, descending towards the bowl of the valley

As he goes, he whistles and shouts alternately, until repetition turns the sounds into an automatic function that he barely notices. He knows the dog will hear nothing. It will have its nose to the wet ground, the wind in its ears, alert only to the smell of sheep or squirrels.

He begins to think of the moment he'll have to tell her that it's gone, remembering the last time it ran off, how her lip curled downwards, trembling. He'll see the same old accusation in her eyes: 'You promised.' Fucking promises. Fucking animal. As he starts down the hillside, it's growing dark. While he scans the landscape, he begins to rehearse the words he'll use to tell her.

Seeing the last of the sun is still lighting the treetops in the valley below, he breaks at intervals into a jog. The darker it gets, the less chance there is of spotting the animal, but it isn't the growing darkness that urges him on now: he's getting closer to the edge of Cramer's land. If the dog makes it as far as the estate, Cramer won't think twice. He's the sort of bastard that keeps his gun by his side, waiting for a chance to use it.

He rarely goes down there these days. He's always preferred the rough heathland on top of the hills. He likes the space, the extremity of the elements. Since his child-hood, he's navigated the expanses between the rock crags that project like islands from the heather and rough grass. It was something his son never understood; born bored, always straining to get away.

Despite the stinging wind, he keeps staring hard into the gloom, his eyes streaming, until almost blind he turns his ankle in a gully. It's only a strain, but it hurts. He limps on as quickly as he can, trying to walk off the pain.

It's slow going until he picks up the rough track that leads down past a barn to the fields in the valley below. It's worth checking. Maybe the dog isn't as stupid as he thought. It might have sensed night coming and taken shelter.

The barn isn't old, but it is in poor repair. Around it, weeds grow up through rusting farm equipment. Blades that once turned the heavy earth wait to be useful again. The door is shut but not locked. Inside, the soft, sweet smells of agriculture mingle with the reek of diesel and engine oil. On the work bench a few hand-tools lie where they were last used, flecked with rust. Their dirty handles look as though they might still hold warmth from the hands that last touched them. The only movement in the barn is a pile of sacks stirred by the breeze from the open door. There is no sign of the dog.

Beyond the barn, ragged fields run towards a wooded area that forms the boundary of Cramer's estate. Hollins scrambles along beside a collapsed wall that follows the edge of a field and, at last, catches sight of the dog. It's trotting along the side of the copse. It stands out briefly in the failing light, a lithe silhouette against a slab of pale rock, before disappearing into the shadows again. He sets off on a course that will intercept the animal at the corner of the wood, before it can reach open farm-land, but when he reaches the tree line, there is no sign of it. He doubles back towards the rise where he last saw it.

As he begins back up the slope he sees, at the edge of the wood, Cramer's Range Rover. It is parked at an angle blocking the track that runs through the trees. Hollins's stomach knots and under his breath he spits the name of his neighbour.

Creeping closer and pushing back branches as he goes, he looks around, desperate to find the dog before Cramer can draw a bead on it. It's darker in the wood, but even in the gloom he can see the bastard's there, standing on the track just ahead. It's too late to dodge him, and maybe it's better not to. Cramer can hardly shoot the dog if he is there with him. At least he can buy time. He steps out of the trees and nods his head almost imperceptibly in greeting. 'Cramer.'

The other man acknowledges him calmly. 'Evening, Hollins. Don't see you down here much these days. You want to be careful sneaking about in the dark. We shoot in these woods. Accidents happen.'

It's difficult to believe that their sons were inseparable, once. Cramer's son helped run the estate now, and he'd inherit it all one day.

As usual Cramer, the gentleman farmer, has a broken shotgun under his arm. 'You looking for something?'

Before Hollins can form a reply, Cramer gestures towards the other side of his Range Rover where the dog is sitting, wet and mud-lashed from its travels, with a look of dejected guilt. A thin rope is strung between its collar and the car's bumper. Cramer points roughly with his gun. 'I should shoot it. It's not the first time.'

'It got out. I come lookin' for it, soon as I could.'

'I can't have it running around worrying my livestock.'

Hollins knows all the estate livestock are safely down in the fields at the bottom of the valley, but he stays silent, glowering in the dark as Cramer continues. 'I could shoot it. It'd be quite legal. I'm within my rights. You're a long way from home. What are you and your animal doing running round my bloody woods anyway?'

The two men stand in silence for a moment, the dog whining quietly. Finally, it is Hollins that speaks.

'It goes looking. For him, I mean. It were his dog.' In an effort to stop his words sounding like a plea, he spits them out like a threat. It is too dark for him to see the other man's face properly, but he sees Cramer shuffle and lower his gaze.

When Cramer speaks again his voice is softer. 'Well, see you keep it under control from now on.' He unties the rope from the bumper and holds it out to Hollins in a leather-gloved hand.

Hollins takes the dog's tether and yanks it toward him, heading immediately towards the edge of the wood. Face set, he walks up the track that will take him out of the trees into the open ground beyond. Behind him, Cramer is saying, 'Can I give you a lift back up to the house? Hollins?' But he keeps walking and doesn't look back. Cramer makes no effort to follow him.

He is tired now and his legs ache. He hates the animal for what it has cost his pride, for the lost hours of work he's spent searching the moor. He hates it for running and for wanting to leave. He pulls the rope hard, and hates the animal even more because of the way it cringes and looks up at him.

As he leaves the track and begins to climb, he can still feel Cramer's eyes on him. Beyond the exposed slopes, a gap in a dry stone wall opens into the narrow lane he has known since childhood. The lane that will take him back to the farmhouse. He pauses before going through the gap. At his feet, the dog shivers. It is dark now. The fell has become one deep blue shadow beneath the last pale glimmer of evening. The lane, cut into a deep trough, crosses the hill to the farmhouse where a solitary light shines in the kitchen window: a single sign of human activity that extends neither warmth nor welcome, but makes the stillness of the other rooms solid and their darkness deeper.

He slumps back against the wall, sinking down into the wet grass, and pulls the dog to him. He draws the animal to his chest and wraps his coat around it. Holding it tightly, he presses his head into the soaked fur of the dog's neck and smells on it the mud and stagnant water of the fell. Beneath the dog's pelt he can hear the surge of the air filling its lungs and, against his cheek he feels the rapid, vital beating of the dog's heart.

Hitler Was an Artist Too

I T's COLD AND wet. Three of us – Alan, Wayne and me – lean on our brooms, smoking thin, hand-rolled cigarettes, trying to simultaneously keep warm and remain inactive. *Minimum wage, minimum effort*; the motto of the unofficial union of Saturday boys.

The smoke-black wall of the Methodist church overhangs the store's back yard, and water from its broken gutter slaps onto the cobbles. We stare at the drizzle-softened posters on the chapel's notice board and, mumbling around his ciggie, Wayne reads their slogans aloud: 'God is Love' and 'Jesus is Coming'. I can see he's building up to a sarcastic comment, but instead he tenses up, wide-eyed, hissing, 'He's coming.'

Alan and I stare at him.

'Bert. Bert's coming.' He nods urgently toward the back door of the store.

Three half-smoked rollies fly over the wall in perfect formation and brooms hiss against the cobbles.

'Morning, Bert.'

'Haven't you lot finished yet? Move yourselves. I've got other things for you to do inside, and I want one of you to clean my car later.'

He considers it a privilege to be allowed to wash his car instead of working in the warehouse. In summer, it is, but today it's freezing so I'm hoping he'll make Wayne do it.

'I hear it's your last day, young man. We'll miss you, won't we, boys.'

Silence. Not because they won't miss me – although they really won't – but because they hate Bert. I sense Alan and Wayne watching me from the corner of their eyes and I feel myself blushing. I haven't told anyone yet, except the office staff.

I have worked here for exactly one year. This, as Bert-the-blurt has kindly announced, is my last day. Damage done, he scuttles back indoors, his bow-legged stride making his torso swing from side to side. 'Get a move on.'

As soon as he's gone, the tobacco and Rizlas come out again.

'Your last day? You kept that quiet, you twat.'

'Gonna cry?'

'Bert will. He loves you.'

I show Alan two fingers. 'Bert's an equal opportunities employer; he hates us all equally.' But I know what he said is true; Bert does like me. He's singled me out from the start, treated me a little differently from the others, ever since he found me sketching on my tea break, sticking his beak over my shoulder. 'Think you're Picasso, do you? It's rubbish, that.' Later on, out of sight of the others, he winked at me. 'Good to have a bright lad like you on the team.'

Even when he caught me skiving off, kipping in one of the sheds, he'd turned a blind eye. The tight-fisted old git docked my wages, but he'd sacked other people for less than that. It'd pissed Wayne off somethin' bad. He didn't speak to me for a fortnight, as though I should've resigned out of a sense of honour. It doesn't really matter; as far as I can tell, it makes fuck all difference whether Bert likes someone or not – we're all doing the same shitty jobs, sweeping, fetching and carrying.

Cleaning the yard takes most of the morning. Later, back inside, I find Bert in the tearoom, where the smell of fag ash, like spent gunpowder, seems to cling to every cup and plate. He's smoking a cig, really going for it, sucking hard and blasting the smoke back out.

He's ignoring me and I him, and I know he's hoping I won't stay long. This is one of his favourite ambush sites. He waits here, with his bony old paws set like traps, for one of the shop girls to wander in. As soon as they reach for a cup, he's on them, hands all over the place. *You're looking very nice today. Pretty as a Renoir. Give your Uncle Bert a cuddle. How about a little kiss? Go on . . .* And they put up with his creeping mitts, afraid they'll get the boot.

I see what he's up to and I hang on, stirring a teabag around my cup slowly, tapping out a tune on the chipped Formica with my fingernails. When Claire comes in, I'm glad I stayed.

As she passes him, she gets a sly hand on her arse, and Bert glances in my direction, dying for me to fuck off. He's hardly the shy type, but he doesn't like to perform in front of an audience. I light a cigarette to show I'm not moving, and he retreats, furious, face like a fist; hard and screwed shut. He can't do anything about it other than snap, 'Hurry up with that fag, young man. I've got things for you to do. I don't care if it is your last day.'

Claire is turned away from me, searching the cupboard for the cleanest cup, but I see her stand a little straighter, pausing for a second before she goes back to her search. I meant to tell her I'm leaving before now. I certainly didn't want her to find out like that.

Bert leaves us. His parting glance tells me I'll pay for it later, but as I put my cold tea on the draining board, Claire smiles at me and it's worth whatever he has in store.

'You going then?' She takes the cigarette from my hand and takes a drag. 'When were you gonna tell me?'

'I meant to. I just didn't get the chance. It's not like I could just call you.'

In the real world we don't meet – outside of this place, our worlds barely touch. Her boyfriend, Craig, is a psycho. Despite the evidence, she doesn't think he is, just 'a bit of a dick occasionally', but just to be on the safe side, I'm forbidden from talking to her outside work. We went on a couple of brief dates in a neighbouring town where we wouldn't be recognised, but that was it. Of course, Darnforth is a small town, so we've bumped into each other once or twice on a Saturday night. She's always with Psycho-Boy and his friends and I was embarrassingly afraid that he would see the glances between us. But even when I knew I might get my head kicked in for it, I still couldn't make myself look away from her, not completely. Compared to everyone else I know in Darnforth, Claire seems like a film star. I know it's all an act, but still . . .

'You in the warehouse this afternoon?'

'Maybe.' She smiles. We both blush a little, even though we've known each other for months. She deliberately stands in my way as I leave, and briefly our bodies make contact as I brush past her. When I leave, it will be Claire that I miss. Only Claire.

Bert watches me washing his car in the rain. I don't look at him, but I can hear the rain drops on his umbrella and, from the corner of my eye, I can see the scuffed toes of his shoes on the cobbles each time I bend to dip the sponge in the bucket. The rain running down the collar of my jacket is cold. The water in the bucket is colder. We've been through this routine a dozen times. He pretends he isn't punishing me, and I pretend I don't care. I know what's on his mind, but I'm nearly finished by the time he says anything.

'Art school, is it? I don't know why you're bothering with all that bollocks. They won't teach you anything. My little granddaughter can paint better than those hippies.'

The first time he told me about his secret life as a painter was back when I first started here and Wayne was still showing me the ropes and helping me navigate the shambolic backrooms of the store. For the uninitiated, finding your way around was no mean feat. Over its long life, the building had been extended, expanded, knocked-through, filled and added-to again, sagging under the weight of wallpaper, paint and tiles – end of line stock, bought on the cheap and sold to the DIYer on a budget.

He found me in one of the storerooms one afternoon. It didn't feel accidental, so I braced myself for a bollocking, or at least a sarcastic question, but all he said was, 'Did I tell you I paint pictures myself?'

'No, Bert,' I said. 'You didn't mention it.'

He showed me photos of his work: views of the canal with livid orange sunsets. There was something miserly in the over-thinned paint washed across the paper's surface. For a while I thought that painting pictures made Bert okay, but when I told Wayne, he raised his eyebrows, his dislike of Bert undiminished. 'Wasn't that how Hitler started out?'

Bert stays for a while, enjoying the moment. I wipe, he talks. As soon as he leaves, I drop the sponge, smoke a fag under the back porch, then head indoors out of the rain. Back on the shop floor, I'm immediately collared by Lindsey and Stella. They spend six days a week competing for control of the wallcoverings and interior-decorating section – known in staff-room power talk as 'IntDec'. I wait while they argue about the stock they want me to bring down from the store rooms above the shop.

Lindsey alternately beams at customers and glowers at Stella, whose facial spasms hint at the conflict raging between her need to please and her inner anger. Gradually a list of instructions is scrawled in pencil onto a torn piece of patterned wallpaper —stock needed, quantities, locations. The list is snatched back and forth as they argue about its contents. *That one's in the back store – No it isn't, its upstairs – Well it shouldn't be. Who put it there? – I did. If I take the delivery I say where it goes – And what if I need to find it? – You can ask . . .*

Avoiding any eye contact or facial expressions that

might be interpreted by one of them as taking a side, I wait patiently, letting the list grow. The longer it gets, the more difficult it will be to find everything on it. It could easily take all afternoon, if I was the kind of employee who would deliberately waste time. While Stella and Lindsey bicker, Claire appears in the aisle behind them, running a marker-pen in and out of her mouth, silently miming a blow job and ducking around the end of the shelves, making me laugh. Stella looks around, sees an empty aisle and turns back to me, lips pursed, and presses the list into the middle of my chest with her thumb, as though she's driving in a drawing pin.

'Wipe that smirk of your face and fetch these down.'

Claire is waiting near the back stairs, pretending to tidy a shelf of light fittings. After a quick look round to check the coast is clear, we go up, skipping the first and second floors, to the attic store where the shelves are slowly collapsing under piles of long-discontinued stock, and ziggurats of piled boxes spill rolls of wallpaper into the narrow gangways. In the farthest room, we climb up into the gap between stacked boxes and the cracked ceiling. Up in the dusty warmth, the cocooning softness of the stacked paper sucks in sound, keeps secrets.

'So obviously, you were gonna mention it?'

'Yeah, of course.' I can feel myself blushing and hope she can't tell in the gloom of the storeroom. I was going to tell her. I meant to. It was just a case of finding the moment.

'I thought you'd decided not to go?

'I changed my mind. Sorry, I meant to . . . It was all a bit last minute.'

'Why sorry. I don't mind. It's up to you.' She pauses,

thinking, then lets out a little laugh. 'You're too late, anyway. Term started in September.'

'They said I could still join . . . if I wanted.'

'Oh.'

'So, you know . . .'

'That's great.' She doesn't sound convinced, and she's avoiding my eyes.

When I reply, I'm not even sure if I'm trying to convince her or myself. 'Yeah, it is, great.'

'Do what you want. I really don't care.'

'I didn't think . . .'

'I'm with Craig anyway. So, it's not like, you know . . .'

'No. I know. I mean, I never thought that . . . about us.'

But I have thought about it. Maybe she has too. When we go there in the afternoons, kissing and messing around, we pretend it's just something we do to get through the tedium of the day, but we talk, making stupid plans of how we'll quit and run away to a different town, better than this one, share a flat. She'll get a job working for a cool record label and I'll be an artist. It was all a joke, something to pass the time, but now I'm leaving without her, it feels different than I imagined it would.

We kiss and I open her coarse, nylon shop coat, pushing it aside. We get as far as rubbing each other through our jeans before Stella's silhouette appears at the door of the storeroom and the noises we're making draw her attention. I put my head over the parapet of cardboard and feign innocence.

'Hello, Stella. I was just looking for that stuff you w—'

'I know perfectly well what you were looking for, and she can come down an' all.'

Stella escorts Claire back down to the shop and I head through to the other storerooms. I still haven't told her, haven't actually said the words. I don't want to say it. When I do it will become final and I'm afraid I will never see her again. In the grey half-light of the attic I feel more alone than I remember feeling for a long time. I wonder, if I asked her, would she come with me, but I know the answer already.

At 5.56 p.m. I stand at the back door with the others, killing time. Like a benevolent shepherd among his flock, Bert wanders among the different huddles, grouped according to rank and department. He looks at his watch and smiles like a saint. There's no more work to be done, but he'd rather cut his own throat than let us out early. Four minutes to go.

Alan and Wayne are quiet, avoiding eye contact, as though I've betrayed them. The others make reluctant conversation as we wait for Bert to release us into the glistening dark. Real life waits just beyond the door – TV dinners in front of Saturday night game shows, football, the pub – and the people we've been confined with all day mean less with each twitch of the clock's hands.

Claire is waiting too, with the other shop girls, a few steps away from where I'm standing. I watch her and she watches me, little glances over the shoulder of the girl she's talking to. I could go over, find some excuse to butt in, but there's nothing we can say to each other in front of everyone else. Even so, I step closer, edging away from Alan and Wayne, extracting myself from their mumbled plans for the weekend. Claire is moving towards me, and then

Bert is between us, shuffling in with the weird little dance that he does when he's in a good mood. He leans in, closer and closer, till I can smell his aftershave, and speaks to me quietly, the way you talk to a fellow conspirator, 'Well young man. Off for a pint with your friends?'

'Not tonight.'

'You could've done well here, young man,' he chuckles. 'You might've had my job one day, if you kept your nose clean.'

I'm still watching Claire, but she's looking away from me now, out of the window at the empty yard. As the last minute of the day ticks away, I think she'll wait for me outside and maybe we can go on one of our dates-that-aren't-dates, but out in the street, beyond the yard gates, I see the familiar shape of Psycho-Boy's BMW. He's waiting for her.

The clock counts down and we all pretend not to watch it, waiting for the moment the door's thrown open and we disperse into the surrounding streets, hurrying away to bus stops and old bangers parked in the back roads. For the first time in my brief career as a warehouse boy, I wish it wasn't home time.

Right, on your way, you lot – Night, Bert – Night – See you tomorrow – Not if I see you first —Oh, give over.

I stand outside for a moment and watch Claire crossing the street. Before she gets into the car, she looks at me across the roof. She smiles at me, one last time, and disappears behind the tinted glass. Bert is behind me. The smoke from one of his cheap cigs billows around me in the cold evening air. 'I expect she'll miss you, even if nobody else will.'

I don't say anything and for a moment we stand together in the doorway.

'Did I ever tell you that I paint pictures?'

He's told me a dozen times, but I still say, 'No, Bert. You never did.' Even he smiles.

'I could've gone to art school if I'd wanted. Waste of time. Well, I suppose you'll be better off out of it. They're not like you and me, the people 'round here. Anyway, you can always come back when you change your mind. Get a proper job an' that. Might take you on here again if we're desperate in the holidays.'

'Nah. You're alright, Bert. I think I'll manage.'

He turns the lights off and goes back inside to set the alarm. 'Well, good luck young man.' He can barely bring himself to say it.

Acknowledgements

SEVERAL OF THE stories in this collection have appeared in magazines and anthologies, sometimes in slightly different versions: 'Sink Rate' was first published in *The Bristol Short Story Prize Anthology Volume 11* (Tangent Books), and later in *The Best British Short Stories 2022* (Salt). 'Shooting Season' was first published in Structo Magazine. 'Downstream the Water Darkens' was published in *The London Magazine*. 'Meadowlands' was published in *New Short Stories 11* (the anthology of the Willesden Herald Short Story Competition). 'Memory System' was first published in the anthology, *From Barcelona to Bihar* (Earlyworks Press). 'The Killing Tree' was published in the anthology of the Lightship Short Story Prize. 'Stay' was published by in *Separations* (The Fiction Desk). A version of 'Hitler Was an Artist Too' was published in *Journey Planner and Other Stories* (Cinnamon Press). I would like to thank the editors of these publications, and the other editors who have supported me and published my stories.

'The Killing Tree' was based on a 2012 Channel 4 News report by Jamal Osman, 'Somali justice: forgiveness, money or execution'.

Acknowledgements

I would like to give a huge and heartfelt thanks to Chris and Jen Hamilton-Emery for picking me for the Salt team. I feel extraordinarily lucky.

I began several of the stories in this collection while studying for an MA at the Department of English and Creative Writing at the University of Chichester. This was enabled by a grant from the AHRC. I remain hugely grateful to both institutions for this opportunity. Thank you Stephanie Norgate, Stephen Mollett, Karen Stevens and Dave Swann and Vicki Heath Silk for your help, advice and good humour, and a special thanks to Alison MacLeod for your generosity and encouragement.

Thanks are long overdue to my fellow writers, Gina Challen, Morgaine Davidson, Annabel Mackenzie, and Hannah Radcliffe, for reading all those early drafts, and your friendship.

Finally, and most importantly, thank you to Grace. Without you, the pages would be empty.